"WHAT'S THAT SMELL?"
(Oh, It's Me.)

50 mortifying situations and how to deal

By Tucker Shaw

who knows now what he should have known then.

DEDICATION:

To all the people who've shared their stories with me, I'm sorry I didn't have this book out when you really needed it. Oh well, maybe next time.

Also to my entire family, nuclear and otherwise.

And most especially to Gramp, who taught me there's nothing in the world better than a good solid laugh.

ALLOY BOOKS
Published by Penguin Group
Penguin Young Readers Group,
345 Hudson Street, New York, New York 10014, U.S.A.

Published by Puffin Books,
a division of Penguin Young Readers Group, 2003

10 9 8 7 6 5 4 3 2 1

Illustrations by Mike Reddy
Cover design by Marci Senders
Interior design by Amy Beadle

 Produced by 17th Street Productions,
an Alloy, Inc. company
151 West 26th Street
New York, NY 10001

ISBN 0-14-250011-9
Printed in the United States of America

Contents

INTRODUCTION

There are shelves and shelves of books out there that promise to help you make your teen years happier, healthier, and more productive. They'll teach you how to feel good about yourself, how to make the most of your future, and how to get and keep friends.

This is not one of those books. This book is about the hell that is teen life and how to survive it in one piece.

So if you're desperate to improve relations with your parents or siblings, or improve your study habits, or repair your self-esteem, this is not the book for you. And if you're hoping to reach your full potential as a useful member of society, put this book back on the rack and get your ass to the self-improvement section. (If you've already bought this, ha ha, sucker.)

If, on the other hand, you need to know exactly what to do to preserve your pride after you've been dumped in public, this is your book. If you gotta find out how to clean up after throwing a party that got way out of control, read on. And if you need tips on how best to handle an accidental body fluid emission during an overzealous make-out session, you've come to the right place.

And most of all, if you're up for totally making fun of yourself, you're in luck.

No doubt about it, being a teen can really suck the big one sometimes. Good thing you've got this book to help ease the suckage. You can thank me later.

Tucker

FAMILY NIGHTMARES

Nothing says "humiliation" like screwing up on the home front and getting busted by your family, who you know you're smarter than. (Just ask anyone who's ever endured the words "I'm disappointed in you.")

What else sucks? Having to endure your crazy, psycho parents, especially when they're allowed out in public. Sure, we love our parents, but could they just disappear under a rock when we want 'em to? Please?

What sucks the most? You can't trade in, upgrade, or otherwise replace your family in any way whatsoever. You're stuck with 'em. (And they're stuck with you.)

Read on.

#1 Dad's Pride and Joy, Toasted

The problem: You've got your permit (not your license) and your parents go away for the weekend. So what the hell, you sneak your dad's beloved 1967 mint-condition cherry red Mustang out for a spin, only to discover—when you rear-end their minivan as you pull into the driveway—your parents returned home early. Damage is minimal, but you're busted.

Your goals: Survival; uninterrupted vehicle rights.

Before you begin: If you think you can make it, and if you are truly willing to never see or speak to your family again, run like hell and never look back. In fact, this technique may be applied to any situation in which you anticipate severe punishment. However, understand that this means that the entire rest of your life will suck a whole lot harder than it does now. So you should probably never do this.

Immediately turn your eyes and head downward. Get comfortable with this position, as you'll be hanging your head in a similar fashion for several months henceforth.

Get out of the car immediately and hand over the keys. Do not sit in the driver's seat and cry. Act as grown-up as possible. This is a potential turning point in your relationship with your parents, and for better or worse, you must face it with bravery, humility, and grace. And without acting like a blubbering idiot. Stand tall, pull yourself together, and wait until later to blubber incessantly.

Do not offer an explanation or excuse for what's occurred. They already know what's occurred. And you don't have a reason that they'd ever buy. Stick to "I'll never let this happen again. Ever. I swear."

Even if you've never used the words "Yes, sir," or "Yes, ma'am" with your parents, now's the time to start. It reminds them that you understand that they are in charge, which they are. You'll be amazed at how impressed they'll be by this, and it could lead to leniency somewhere along the painful road ahead.

Do not start offering to pay for any damages, however minor. They might take you up on the offer, and you can't afford it.

Inevitably, one or both parents will want to "discuss" the situation with you. Do not try to weasel out of responsibility (see rule #3), but your best line of defense is to appeal to your dad's ego and his adoration for the car in question. Something along the lines of, "I just love this car so much, and I guess I let my Mustang love get in the way of my judgment. This car . . . our spirits are connected. Do you know what I mean, Dad? Fathers in general are remarkably easily moved by sentimentality, especially when it comes to their cars. (Note: You should probably have your "I love this car!" speech written and rehearsed before ever eyeing the car or jingling the keys in your hand in the first place.)

7   **Suck it up** and accept your punishment, no matter what it is. Anything up to and including house arrest until graduation would be appropriate. And besides, after time, they'll ease up.

The bottom line: *Don't take the car out in the first place. And definitely don't go joyriding to show it off to your friends. No one believes it's yours, anyway.*

Four Ways to Kill Time While Under Legitimate House Arrest

Waste endless hours chatting on AOL. It's the most efficient time-burner going.

Rearrange your room. A few times.

Make dinner. (Hey, you've got nothing better to do, and this will get you out earlier.)

Do all that extra credit you never got to. Then do more. (A surefire sentence-reducer!)

#2 Dangerous Liaisons

The problem: An unbearably hot stepsibling moves into your house. And flirts with you. And you're tempted to flirt back.

Your goal: To defuse the time bomb that this is.

Before you begin: It's important to recognize that even if all your attempts to resist this fatal attraction should fail (and there may be many, many attempts to resist), people from your family to people you don't even know will be completely grossed out. Keep that in the front of your mind for as long as the attraction persists.

1 **Tell someone** you trust. You'll need the support, and plenty of reminders about how potentially sticky things could get, as you navigate these sharky waters. Besides, the added side effect of making your best friend nauseous may help you resist.

2 **Distract yourself** with another crush (or crushes). Set up dates with others. Now more than ever is a good time ask out one of your backups.*

3 **Find someone** to date your stepsibling. Do not hook him/her up with a close friend, as your friendship will inevitably suffer and expire. Instead nudge your stepsibling toward an acquaintance, someone at a safe distance. Preferably the school slut/player. That way, you'll have more ammo: Not only would you never hook up with your stepsibling (right?), you'd never hook up with someone who hooked up with (insert name here)!

4 **Focus** all your attention on his/her most annoying habits. Be alert to toe picking, phone hogging, remote control offenses, dandruff, surreptitiously borrowed T-shirts or baseball caps, snoring, off-key singing, repeated phrases like "Do fries go with that shake?" or "Cornholio!", hair obsessions, etc. Even if a particular habit doesn't particularly skeeve you, use the power of suggestion: You can convince yourself that anything's gross if you try hard enough.

5 **Do not fall** into the classic "just this once" trap. "Just this once" is actually defined in most major colloquial dictionaries as "the beginning of a habit." (Same goes for wearing overalls or smoking cigarettes.)

The bottom line: *Don't hook up with your stepsibling. It's just icky.*

*Note: Multiple crushes are always encouraged at all times, whether you have a significant other or not. Not only do they provide alternative material when your current make-out partner fails to engage you, but they can be drawn on for backup dates, invoked to encourage jealousy, and, in this case, they provide clear and present targets to aim for while retreating from the home front. Besides, your friends would rather spend all day talking about your crushes than your boyfriend.

#3 The Talk, Twisted

The problem: You have a heart-to-heart with Mom (or some other parental type) about sex, and she makes you promise to wait until marriage. But then she finds your birth control pills or condoms.

The goal: To get Mom off your back ASAP.

Before you begin: Understand that this has the potential to mushroom into a several-day affair, a serious test of endurance for even the most patient offspring. One, you've got to get through "The Talk," which in itself can be horrifying, hilarious, disturbing, and anticlimactic, all at the same time. Two, you've got to talk your way out of a big fat lie.

Part I: The Talk.

1 **Remember**, this is a "talk," not a conversation. All you need to do is listen. Don't say too much, just nod at the appropriate times and perhaps mumble, "I see," or "Okay, I understand," at appropriate junctures. Remember, this talk is for her, not you. You already know all this stuff, anyway. (Note: If you don't already know this stuff, ask now. And be sure to follow up with some reliable research because chances are Mom won't be giving you all the dirty details, which you really should know if you're having sex. I mean, seriously.)

2 **Bite the inside** of your cheek, if need be, to keep from laughing when she says things like "making love" or "climax."

3 **Do what you can** to make it a one-on-one talk. One parent is enough because two parents will probably just confuse each other, not to mention you. If possible, get a parent of your own gender to do the honors.

4 **Don't ask** follow-up questions. Feign attentiveness, but do not encourage any extra discussion.

5 **Don't work** on convincing your parent that you're being smart about sex. They're not ready to hear it yet. Besides, most parents will figure this out for themselves once they get over the initial shock.

Part II: Talking your way out of deception.

Face it, if she discovers birth control pills or condoms in your bedroom, you're pretty much busted. But all is not lost. Learn these seven retorts, or appropriate variations, as a precaution before she discovers your contraband. Consider the pros and cons of each in regard to your particular situation (i.e., what you think moms will fall for), and employ them as necessary.* Remember to use only one at a time, and above all, stick to your story.

(Key: C = applicable for condoms, male or female variety. P = applicable for birth control pills. O = applicable for other forms of birth control, including diaphragms, jellies, foams, etc.)

a. "They're not mine. They're (insert name of school slut here)'s!" C, P, O

b. "I heard they help keep your periods regular." P

c. "Okay, I admit it, I wanted bigger boobs and (see above) told me this is the best way." P

d. "I haven't had sex, but I wanted to be safe just in case I fall in love and elope before being able to get my birth control prescription filled. Not that I would ever elope without inviting you and Dad along." C, O

e. "There's some ad on TV that says these pills clear up acne. Are they birth control pills, too? No way! How does my skin look?" P

f. "Oh, those? Um, well, this is kind of embarrassing, but we were going to blow them up and fill that annoying kid's car up with them. But it's okay 'cause we already decided not to!" C

g. "Alex and Pat were at this Safety First! rally the other day and they gave them to everyone there! Can you believe that? They must have left them here or something!" C

h. "See? I knew you'd freak! That's why I can't talk to you about anything! You just don't understand me! At least I'm being responsible!" P, C, O

i. "I happen to know you and Dad had sex when you were my age." P, C, O

The bottom line: *Remember, no matter what the rules are, your choices about sex are yours. So make them good ones.*

*I can't guarantee that these won't blow up in your face. But at this point, you're already busted, so things probably couldn't get all that much worse, anyway. Besides, the chances that they'll work are the best chances you've got.

#4 Unwelcome Intruders

The problem: Dad (or Mom) marries someone who, after much careful consideration, you've decided you just can't stand.

The goal: To survive in peace with as little engagement as possible.

Before you begin: Be certain you can't stand him/her. It's just as likely that you'll end up really getting along if you're open to it. Stepfamily members can be among the most entertaining people in the home and have in many cases proved to be invaluable allies, not to mention incredible friends.

1 **Play nice.** Don't inspire your new enemy to become aggressive. Your goal here is not to destroy or sabotage the situation.

2 **Be selectively honest** about your feelings with others. Telling your freshly married parent exactly how you feel might inspire him or her to attempt to bring everyone closer together, which is antithetical to your goal.

3 **Stake out** your turf. Your turf includes your room, your ride, your favorite space on the couch, etc. Shared spaces are to be used only sparingly.

Be as polite as possible. Remaining civil will help keep the peace, and will give the appearance that you're unfazed by the new arrival, which is exactly what you want them to believe.

Calculate how much time you have until you're outta there, and keep focused on that light at the end of the tunnel.

Do not introduce this person to your friends. You run the risk of having your friends like them, which will confuse the issue profoundly.

Do not borrow their clothes, their shampoo, their car, or anything else.

For daily functions, keep your distance without explicitly revealing your intent. (Note: Your intent will be clear, as these actions certainly speak louder than words.) For example:

a. Laundry: Be willing to transfer your stepparent's laundry to the dryer, but do not accede to folding dried clothes.

b. Bathroom time: Take your sweet, sweet time in the bathroom, acknowledging but effectively ignoring any entreaties to speed up.

c. Meals: Limit your conversational contribution to "No, thank you" and "May I be excused?" Lobby friends for meals at their homes whenever possible. Remarkably, "I'm not hungry" gets you out of forced mealtime more than you might expect. Agree to perform all required meal-related chores . . . but, do not agree to "teaming up" (i.e., "You wash, I'll dry. . . .").

d. Overnight trips or vacations: Bring many more extra Discman batteries than you think you'll need. This will be your best defense.

Five ways to say, "You annoy me," without saying, "You annoy me"

Forget his/her birthday, even when reminded.

Don't comment on his/her new haircut.

Snicker whenever they leave the room, and say, "Nothing," when they ask what's so funny.

Make them call you for dinner several times. When they get frustrated and start knocking on your door, say, "I'm sorry, I didn't hear you." Do this every single night.

Make their dog love you more than them.

#5 Tornado Alley

The problem: You throw a raging party while your parents are away for the weekend . . . and the house gets trashed beyond belief.

The goal: Rescue, recovery, and a seamless return to the "before."

Before you begin: Was it a good party? That's the most important thing. Pat yourself on the back.

1. **Call** your coconspirators* as soon as you wake up. (And wake up early.) They will help you clean. Or else they suck.

2. **Brew a pot** of coffee. You'll need your senses on high alert.

3. **Open all** windows, no matter how cold it is outside, and leave them open for as many hours as you can. The house needs a thorough air transfusion.

4. **Start with** the obvious: Remove all cans, bottles, boxes, or other beverage receptacles to a recycling bin at least one block from your house.

5. **Next**, find and remove all cigarette butts and other smoking remnants.

(Not that you smoke, but sometimes annoying people do. Remember that these guys hide—scour your entire home.

6 **Check for** condoms, wrappers, and the like. Then check again.

7 **Empty trash** to preparty levels. Create new trash if necessary— receptacles should appear natural, as if you'd been there alone all weekend scarfing Entenmann's and drinking diet Squirt.

8 **Wash** any linens you think might need washing. Then, after replacing them on beds, roll around on them a little so they don't smell too fresh. Convincing your parents that you spent the weekend doing their laundry just won't wash. Pun intended.

9 **Inspect** garage and cars. Inspect yard. Check roof, basement, porches, etc. There's no telling where people hid to make out or whatever.

10 **Vacuum** entire home more than once, and walk around a lot afterward. A freshly vacuumed floor will arouse suspicion.

11 **Get a friend**, someone who didn't show at the party, to come over to perform a housewide sniff test. You'll need someone whose senses are keener than yours.

12 **Clear out** the caller ID. It's just smart.

13 **Pay off** any siblings or neighbor children who might have witnessed the festivities.

14 **Be certain** your stereo and television volume controls are turned down.

If your parents flip on NPR and it blows the speakers because the knob was already turned up to 10, it will totally tip them off.

15 **Replace** any soft drinks or snacks that were consumed, minus what you would normally have eaten. If there's too much fresh food in the house, red flags will rise.

16 **Check and refill** booze bottles. Not to imply that you drank or served alcohol (because you didn't, right?), but bad party guests often snoop their way into the liquor cabinet. Use water if necessary to bring bottles back up to preparty levels, but don't dilute so far that liquor's integrity is compromised.

17 **Take a massive** shower. Wash everything. Floss, deep condition your hair, clean your ears. Hydrate thoroughly. Cleaning house includes cleaning yourself.

The bottom line: Stay in control of your party, from the moment you conceive of doing it to the moment you finish cleaning up the house. Do not let things get out of control. That means keeping the guest list small and the refreshments to a minimum, closing up shop on the early side, and not overindulging.

*Note: Never, ever throw a party alone. It's just not fair, effective, efficient, or wise. Always recruit at least four people. And remember, the law of party-giving says that if your guest list includes thirty people, you'll either get eleven or you'll get ninety, and there's no guaranteed formula for figuring out which way it will go.

#6 Unapproved Guests

The problem: Your boyfriend or girlfriend sneaks in after your parents have crashed, and a younger sibling blackmails you, threatening to tell on you.

The goal: To minimize leaks and prevent future ones.

Before you begin: Remember that dealing with your siblings is different than dealing with anyone else in the world. You can't apply the same logic, sensitivity, or reason that would make sense when dealing with other people. Only you know your sib's buttons and exactly how to push them most effectively. (Your sib also knows this about you, which is why you're in this situation in the first place.)

Bargain, negotiate, and bribe, bribe, bribe. Consider carefully what will be most enticing and figure out what you can deliver that would put the kibosh on the situation most effectively. The top variable is your sibling himself/herself. Does he/she want access to your car? Has he/she also committed an offense and now needs protection? It pays to know and understand siblings' wants and needs at all times.

2 **Get him/her in** on the whole deal. Making him/her an accessory not only guarantees your sib's silence (your sib will be equally culpable if you're caught) but it also might make him/her feel more important socially. (Caveat: Be careful when making an offer to this effect. It can, and will, backfire if he/she is uninterested in furthering his/her social status. For example, if he/she is actually cooler or more popular than you are.)

3 **Promise future protection** should he/she wish to break a similar rule. Make the promise solid, but do not write it down. Such physical evidence can be damning during a future episode.

4 **Threaten to tell** everyone at school that your sib (fill in the blank with something ill and embarrassing like "wears a wrestling suit to bed" or "worships Aaron Carter" or something equally socially disastrous).

5 **This may sound** like common sense, because it is, but I'm gonna say it, anyway: In the future, take greater care to ensure a clean entry and getaway. In short, don't be stupid enough to get busted. In addition, cast a wider net for hookup locations.

The bottom line: Remember, siblings are special. The reason you don't have to follow the rules with your sibs is because at the end of the day, you're still gonna have dinner at the same table (or whatever), and—be honest—you wouldn't want it any other way.

Perfect Sneak-ins: Here's how to guarantee a boyfriend or girlfriend's visit without detection:

Do it not when everyone's asleep, but when everyone's awake. The more action in the house, the more likely they are to not be noticed.

Make sure he/she is in sneakers, not boots.

Prehoard bottles of water and snacks in your room. Kitchen visits are dangerous in the extreme.

Same goes for bathroom visits, so pee first.

Keep your radio and/or TV going while he/she is there to muffle your own voices.

#7 Age-Inappropriate Behavior

The problem: You've just picked up a copy of the new CD by your favorite new group, but just as you start to unwrap it so you can play it in your car's stereo in the CD store parking lot, your mom pulls up next to you, blasting the exact same CD you just bought . . . and rocking out, hard. In fact, other people in the lot are looking.

The Goal: To allow parental freedom of choice, while not having to witness it.

Before you begin: Not as many people are looking as you think. Still, this is an egregious infraction on the parent-child relationship, which is marked in nature by, among other things, drastically different taste in music. It's just how life is supposed to go. Therefore, do not underestimate the seriousness of this situation.

1 **Stop unwrapping.** You're probably going to need to take the CD back.

2 **Get out** of there, quick. Key in the ignition, shift to reverse, and hit the first pedal from the right. Even if she sees you and/or yells after you, split the scene. Pronto.

3 **Immediately disavow** your love for the band or artist in question. Remove any posters, T-shirts, or other promotional merchandise from your room. Give any other CDs by the same artist to your younger siblings.*

4 **Later**, when Mom tries to bond with you over the music (perhaps in the context of getting mad at you for laying serious rubber while trying to get away from her in the parking lot), tell her you think it sucks, no matter how you felt about it before busting her.

The bottom line: Believe it or not, your parents choices don't reflect as significantly on you as you think they do.

*Note: This will have the extra-added-bonus effect of providing you with more anti-younger-sibling artillery for the next time you need it. I mean, they like the same music as your mom! Ew!

#8 on the Spot

The problem: Uncle Mark is getting married. The sucky part? You've gotta make a toast in front of the entire rehearsal dinner party. And to be honest, speaking in public is one of your biggest fears.

The goal: To perform under pressure.

Before you begin: When they tell you that it's an honor to have been asked to do this, they mean it. Shut up and do it. You can't weasel out.

Decide what to say

a. Figure out exactly who you're giving the toast to. Will you direct your comments to Mark and his soon-to-be significant other? Or will you be speaking more generally, to the entire room? (Of course, everyone will hear you no matter what you choose, but it helps to think of someone specific at the receiving end of your wit when you're trying to figure out which direction to go in.)

b. Give them what they want to hear. Contrary to popular belief, most wedding audiences don't like surprises; they like to hear what they expect to hear. Remember, you're doing this for the engaged, not for yourself. You're to make Uncle Mark feel good about himself. Sure, a little jab here or there can be fun, but your speech must strike a positive note.

2 Write it up

a. Write down all the things you think you might want to say, then cut it down to one. Any more than that and people will get bored. Promise.

b. Don't write a poem or sing an original song or anything overly ambitious like that. Unless you're Sting, which you aren't. Stick to clever prose.

c. Don't tell any embarrassing second- or thirdhand stories about the newlyweds as children. Someone will already have this covered. Besides, odds are you weren't even alive when Uncle Mark was a kid. Unless you're from the South. Or Maine.

3 Practice, practice, practice

a. Work on your breathing. Practice standing still, without fidgeting, and completely filling your lungs. See how slowly you can let the air out. Practice saying the alphabet, without rushing, in one breath. Get used to keeping your lungs as full as possible and not rushing while you speak.

b. Work on memorizing what you're going to say. You can have notes to refer to if you must, but this is borderline lame, and the more you know by heart, the more people will think you're speaking from the heart.

c. Use the buddy system: Get someone to listen to you practice several times before the event. Be certain this person has your best interests at heart and would reap no benefit from seeing you screw up royally. Have him/her promise in blood that he/she will be brutally honest with you.

Deliver

a. Don't wear anything too tight around your neck. If you must wear a tie or scarf, make sure it's fastened correctly, leaving your air vents clear and open. Also, break in the shoes you're going to wear, and get used to them. Nothing sucks worse than being distracted by uncomfortable shoes.

b. Do not initiate the moment with a clinking on a glass. Let someone else do that. Who knows? With any luck, they'll forget, and you'll be off the hook.

c. Drink a warm beverage before you speak. It'll enrich and deepen your voice, and it makes you sound sexier.

d. Use the first three words to assess the acoustics and your volume, and adjust your sound level accordingly. You want to be loud enough to be heard, but not so loud that you're annoying.

e. Do not spit. I mean, really. Watch the spittle. No one wants to see that.

f. Even though you may have memorized what you want to say, leave yourself open for improv if the opportunity presents itself. As always, when improvising, be 100 percent sure what you're about to say is actually funny before you say it.

g. Do not go to a question-and-answer period.

> **The bottom line:** Remember that no one was really paying attention to what you were saying, anyway. They were only paying attention to what you were wearing. So make sure you look good, and don't piss anyone off. You'll score major, major points.

#9 Parental Fashion Faux Pas

The problem: You've been looking forward to the class ski trip since you heard about all that went down at last year's. Too bad your dad heard many of the same stories . . . because he's now signed up to be one of the parental chaperons. This is bad enough, but on day one, he's rocking a neon orange one-piece ski suit that probably should have been destroyed in the early eighties. And not only that, it's giving him an obvious wedgie.

The goal: To distance yourself from embarrassing relatives and to reestablish your own position at the top of the fashion ladder.

Before you begin: Understand that your deepest fears are, in fact, true—situations like this can profoundly affect your social life. At least for a day or so.

1 **Distance yourself** from Dad, as soon as possible. You will not be skiing with him today.

2 **Don't mention** the ski suit to your friends. They already saw it. If you're lucky, they feel sorry for you. If they bring it up, roll your eyes and change the subject to, perhaps, your own flawless taste and how it's being exhibited in today's outfit.

3 **If you come across** your dad on the slopes, hide. This may sound cruel, but let's face it, it's necessary. The worst thing you can do is to acknowledge your embarrassment or, worse, tell your dad to go back to the lodge to change. This will only egg him on, and he's liable to show up in something even more awful tomorrow.*

4 **Acknowledge** that some people will think your dad is really cool. Question whether these people should really be your friends.

5 **Stage a mission** to collect and destroy the offensive snowsuit. Yes, this may seem like sabotage. That's because it is.

6 **If you can stomach** the notion, offer to shop with Dad for his next ski outfit and select something understated, classic, to your own impeccable taste. Remember, walking fashion disasters don't need our anger, they need our help. Allow him to wear a nutty hat, if he must.

7 **Make sure**, for the next several weeks, that your own looks are tight, every single day. Your prime response to familial fashion disasters is to chart your own stylish course and stick to it.

The bottom line: *Your best defense against this kind of embarrassment is to not make an issue out of it. You won't win, so why fight? Besides, if you want your parents off your back about what you wear, which you do, then you've gotta give them the same props.*

*Note: Since the dawn of time it's been true: Parents LIVE to embarrass their kids. Whether it be by being annoying in public situations (think tacky outfits, stupid jokes) or by setting you up to be embarrassed on your own (remember the year they made you go as a bunny for Halloween?) or by rocking an age-inappropriate look (knee-high boots at your soccer game) or even by really getting into your music (when Dad knows the words to *NSYNC songs, you've got a real problem on your hands). Understand that this problem will continue to arise, time after time, until long after you've left home.

LOVE SUCKS

Ah, love. Yep, you know, that thing that makes your heart beat and your pits sweat at the same time. Face it, there's nothing more humiliating than being embarrassed by, or in front of, a crush.

Enjoy!

#10 Misplaced Affections

The problem: Your crush, the hottest hottie in town, isn't flirting back tonight. In fact, he doesn't even notice you. That is, until you decide to kiss someone else at the party.

The goal:
Damage control.

Before you begin: It's imperative that you do not panic. Believe it or not, you can turn this to your advantage. It has been shown, in clinical studies, that jealousy in situations like this can make you more desirable to your crush.

1 **Don't ditch**, outright, whoever you were caught kissing for the duration of the evening. Dissing him/her in hopes of hooking up with your crush that same evening will make you seem desperate. Not to mention, any self-respecting crush wouldn't want to get near you right after you've been making out with someone else. That's just gross. Just get out of the shadows and back into the party—with your posse.

2 **Don't avoid** your crush for the rest of the evening, but don't give him/her too

much attention, either. Return, as quickly as possible, to a comfortable, friendly vibe, like the one that should have existed before you got busted. And don't freak out if he/she hooks up with someone else the same evening. After all, fair is fair.

3   **Let your** new kissing partner down gently, but completely. Make it clear that you're not releasing him in favor of your real crush, even if that is the truth. (Never burn your bridges—you might need the backup someday.)

4   **Early** the following week, at school, make certain the grapevine (i.e., your friends and allies, as well as your crush's) understands where your true crush energy lies. (Without, of course, dissing your make-out buddy.) After planting the seed that you're still into him/her, let it be. Never bring up the situation again. No apologies, no excuses. This will make you appear more confident about the situation than you are, which will make you more attractive in your crush's eyes.

5   **If necessary**, release your crush and move on, understanding that this situation may be irreparable and that it's possible the best you could hope for is to learn a valuable lesson and be done with it. (What's more, appearing like you plumb don't care that much makes you more attractive in general, which is a plus no matter who you're crushing on.)

> ***The bottom line:*** Your best defense here is, of course, not to go off making out with some second-rate crush at a random party in the first place. Remember, sometimes it's okay to go a party and not hook up. In fact, most of the time, it's a whole lot better that way.

#11 Rejection Close to Home

The problem: Your crush of five years says no, hard, when you ask him/her out. But then he/she hooks up . . . with your younger sibling!

The solution: To reduce the humiliation you are certainly, and justifiably, feeling.

Before you begin: Remember, revenge can certainly be fun, but it's much smarter to move on to better things. Use this as your mantra: "He/she sucks and I can do better." Repeat this to yourself over and over until you believe it. (Note: Stick to it, 'cause convincing yourself could take a while.) Then take the high road and sidestep the gutter.

First things first: Do not draw any more attention to this situation, if at all possible. If your sibling doesn't know about your crush, thank your lucky stars and zip your trap. Remember, a clean break for yourself here is worth way more to your peace of mind (not to mention your cooler-than-thou factor, which needs all the help it can get) than a messy situation for everyone.

2 **Distance matters.** Even if you're not certain that your sibling knows you have/had a crush on the crushee in question, assume that they do and decide you will not make an effort to bond with your sibling for the foreseeable future. Inform him/her or not of your silentish treatment at your own discretion; however, understand that he/she is persona non grata for now. Do not let him/her see you sweat. Stick to this—the emotional shrapnel that was once your pride will thank you.

3 **Should your sibling** take the case beyond the family, for example, to tell your friends about the situation, laugh it off with a wave. "As if!" comes in very handy here.

4 **Do not**, however, cease speaking to your crush if you already have a "speaking" relationship. Business as usual outside the home. The last thing you want or need is for him/her to think you give a rat's ass about the situation, which will just make you look pathetic.

5 **Avoid**, at all costs, seeing them together in a situation where etiquette would dictate a verbal exchange. No one can expect you to resist making cutting remarks, but the truth is, they won't help anyone. Comments like "You deserve each other" won't help. Remember, pathetic is not a particularly attractive quality to strive for.

6 **Do not attempt** to sabotage their relationship in any way. It's not worth the potential backfire, and besides, you've moved on from this situation. Right?

7 **Never, ever**, under any circumstances, consent to an appearance on any television talk show, daytime or otherwise, that seeks to exploit your unusual situation. These will not bring you fame or accolades; they will only embarrass you in front of the country, then spit you out. No matter how right you are.

8 **Lobby for** your own telephone line, if you don't have one yet. There is no pleasant or gracious way to answer the phone, only to have it be your crush looking for your kid sibling.

9 **Get back** on the horse, and find another crush, pronto (see page 10 for why it's important to have more than one crush at a time).

10 **If**, in the future, it becomes clear that your crush actually wants to be with you instead of your sibling, do not submit. Dating your sibling's ex is universally considered pretty desperate and is to be avoided at all costs. Unless, of course, you really are soul mates, in which case you won't pay any attention to this advice, anyway.

11 **Treat yourself** to the most extensive makeover you can afford and/or muster. Not so that your crush will realize what he/she's missing, but to help yourself upgrade to a higher class of crush next time around. A little light shopping and a professional haircut may be all you need.

The bottom line: There are no words emphatic enough to describe how completely you need to let this go and move on. There is no way you'll ever come out of this looking good—or, more important, feeling good—if you don't cut your losses and get out of the situation as soon as possible.

#12 Delicate Declarations

The problem: You fall for your best friend. So you decide to ask him/her out. He/she acts disgusted, laughs, or worse, stops hanging out with you.

The goal:
To erase the event as completely as possible.

Before you begin: *When asking someone out, it usually pays to make it as simple and vague as possible, at least until you've figured out whether you really like each other or not. "Hey, you wanna go grab dinner with some people this weekend?" is much easier to play off than "I've liked you ever since the second grade, and our love is eternal, and I believe we belong together, truly, madly, deeply."*

1. **Keep the episode** between you two. Tell no one. To this end, understand that you must, MUST pop this kinda question in person or on the telephone. Never, EVER declare a risky love in writing. Hard evidence can, and probably will, come back to haunt you.

2. **Try this**, when he/she laughs in your face: "Yeah, right. You know you've been all over me for months."

3. **Or turn it around:** "You believed me? I'm so sure!!" It works.

4. **Deny, deny, deny.** "What are you talking about? I never said that!" may not convince him/her, but the rest of the world may not be wise to it.

5. **Get another BF/GF**, pronto. Preferably someone your intended knows well. Nothing says "I don't care" like hooking up with his/her best friend.

6. **Don't extinguish** your flame entirely. This rejection might only be his/her initial reaction. In time, perhaps he/she will see that you two belong together.

The bottom line: You knew there was a risk, so there's really no injustice here. Broken hearts happen every day. Not that that makes it easier, but know that you're in good company. Having your heart broken is an inevitable fact of life.

Note: Smart intelligence-gathering techniques can keep this situation from spinning wildly out of control. But never, ever fish for specific information, like, "Does he/she like me?" This will get back to your crush. Instead, ask more generically for advice from a third party, like, "Do you think he/she is cute?" and see where that takes you. You'll likely get the answers you're looking for.

#13 When You Make Three

The problem: You hook up with a hot guy/girl . . . then find out he/she has a GF/BF, the hard way. That is, when the GF/BF busts you two making out.

The goal: To maintain as much dignity as possible in this undignified situation.

Before you begin: Clinical research shows that most third parties involved in illicit hookups (i.e., you) actually did know they were treading on dangerous ground. Don't be this kind of sucker in the first place. And definitely don't believe it if he/she tells you they're "going to" break up or that he/she is planning to leave the GF/BF anytime soon. It's unlikely that this is true, and even if it is, he/she should take care of that business before getting all up in yours, don't you think?

1 **Figure out** how best to get out of there, fast. You've had your action; it's time to roll. This is way more than you bargained for. As innocent as you may be to the situation, you may still be a target for a jealous lover. The smartest thing you can do is be a moving target, which is way tougher to hit.

2 **See step #1.**

3 **Consider making** the point, loudly, that you didn't know any better, but don't let that impede you in your swift getaway. Believe me, you don't want to watch the fight that's about to ensue.

4 **On the way out**, say something really rude to your ex-make-out buddy, like, "Omigod, I just kissed you? I thought you were someone else! Ew! Ew!" Again, however, don't let this outburst get in the way of your speedy exit.

5 **Perform damage control** with your posse by coming clean about the situation. Focus on how you've been wronged.

6 **Don't ever speak** to this person again. Unless, of course, you're truly eternal soul mates, in which case you need to wait for him/her to clear him-/herself of all other involvements before even considering accepting any apologies.

Bottom line: *Do whatever you can to not find yourself in this situation in the first place. Do your research before hooking up, and if you have any notion that your intended mack is already taken, don't go there.*

#14 Thespian Alert

The problem: Your crush from afar, the one from some other school who finally introduces him-/herself after months of you guys checking each other out at the mall coffee shop, asks you out, and you say yes. To your horror, on that first date, you find out he/she is like the biggest thespian at his/her school. President of the drama club and founder of the Gilbert and Sullivan Society (GASS). The thing is, you can't stand actors.

The goal: To end the madness before it begins.

Before you begin: Consider whether your pet peeve about actors is reasonable or not. Sure, they can be annoying, but so can you. Actors are people, too.

1 **Keep your cool** through the rest of the evening. While you may be tempted to scream, "What? An actor?" at the top of your lungs, perhaps clearing the table with your forearm in the process and smashing all the dishes on the floor, don't do it. (If your reaction is truly this dramatic, you should consider becoming an actor yourself, you drama queen/king.)

2 **Don't kiss** good night. Not even just this once.

3 **Okay**, maybe just this once. But never again.

4 **Do not call** the next day, and do not accept a phone call from the crush in question. If you're lucky, they're not into the whole thing, either; and before you know it, the whole thing could just fade sweetly and silently away.

5 **If your date** does call, twice, you're required to call back and tell the truth.* Do this as quickly and simply as possible, leaving no room for misinterpretation. Do not agree to another date. (Unless the whole acting thing takes off and they get a starring role in their own WB angst drama.)

The bottom line: Give it a chance. Who knows, maybe this actor is different. Besides, what does it say about you that you've been hot for an actor this whole time?

*Note: "The truth" in this instance does not mean saying, "Well, you're really cute, but I hate actors." It means saying something more like, "Gee, I had a really great time with you, but I don't think we should take it any further."

#15 Emissions Disasters

The problem: All you were doing was making out, but you/he totally ejaculated!

The goal: To get past it without sabotaging future sessions.

Note: *The best way to avoid an unwanted emission is not to place yourself in a situation that could lead to one in the first place. But since these situations can come up, so to speak, when we least expect them, we all know that's impossible. Therefore, your best bet, as the ejaculator, is to lower your levels as much as you can well in advance of the make-out session. Trust me. If you need tips on how to do that, you're in the wrong book. (We're PG-13 here.)*

For the ejaculator:

1. **Excuse yourself** to the bathroom, immediately. You'll need a moment alone to pull yourself together. Wash your hands, and other extremities, twice.

2. **Admit** what just happened and laugh, together.

3. **Date over.** Head home.

4. **Tell no one**, or else exaggerate wildly, understanding that no one will believe you.

For the ejaculatee:

1. **Excuse yourself** to the bathroom, immediately. (Not the one that the ejaculator is in.) You'll need a moment alone to collect yourself. Wash your hands, twice.

2. **Say nothing.**

3. **Laugh** with the ejaculator, if he brings it up.

4. **Date over.** Head home.

5. **Call a friend**, take a deep breath, and scream, "Ewwwwwwwwwwwwwwwwwwwwwwww," as loud as possible.

The bottom line: Remember, even if it's gross, a fully clothed ejaculation is the safest kind there is. So don't panic.

#16 Self-intimacy, Interrupted

The problem: You get busted masturbating in your car. By your crush.

The goal: To make it go away. And to make certain it never, ever happens again. Ever.

Before you begin: What were you thinking!?

1 **Never apologize**, never explain. In fact, don't say anything at all. Seriously. I mean, there's nothing to say, really. All your cards are already on the table, and there's no way to explain this one away. This is a good thing, because words only make situations like these even worse. Play your cards right, and you should never have to address this incident out loud again.

2 **Promise yourself** that you'll never forget this moment, because this is a lesson you really need to learn. Public self-gratification is exactly the

kind of habit that you don't want to get into.

3 **Abandon all hope** of ever hooking up with the crush who busted you. Sure, maybe he/she will be understanding and cool about it, but the chances are, let's face it, pretty slim.

4 **Hold your head** (the one on your shoulders) up high. The rumor that you're into autoerotica (in every sense of the word) is probably out there, but that doesn't mean you have to acknowledge it.

5 **In the future**, make an effort to speed things up a little! The longer these things take, the more likely it is you'll be busted.

6 **Remember:** Everyone masturbates. But not everyone gets caught. Smarten up already, and don't do it in your car! Duh!

The bottom line: Understand that there is a time and place for this activity, and limit yourself in the future to appropriate locations. Appropriate: In bed, with the door locked, preferably at night. Inappropriate: At the back of the bus, in the closet at school, behind the field house, in your crush's bathroom, under the bleachers, in the car, etc.

#17 Poorly Styled Prom Dates

The problem: You've been waiting for MONTHS for the prom, even hand-selected the hottest date available. That is, you thought your date was on the hot list until he/she arrives at your door (or vice versa) . . . in the most hideous getup you've ever laid eyes on.

The goal: To find some inner grace (under intense pressure).

Before you begin: *Remind yourself that you DO, in fact, have a date to the prom. Things could be much worse. You could be sitting home alone watching other people have fun on* The Real World. *And yes, believe it or not, that would be worse.*

1 **Convince yourself** of the un-self-convinceable: One day you'll look back at this and laugh.* Even if it doesn't prove to be true in the future, it's just about all you have to hang on to.

2 **Make note**, also, that his or her outfit means nothing more than that he or she is wearing a bad outfit and that he or she had a lapse in fashion sense. It is NOT a direct reflection on you or your taste. You'll have ample time to overanalyze this situation (e.g., "But . . . what does this say about US?!?!") tomorrow. But right now, it's prom night, and you've got some freak to get on.

3 **Bite your tongue** and say, "You look great!" Unless pressed, refrain from commenting on the outfit at all.

4 **Get it out** of your system. Excuse yourself for a moment to call a friend for support, run upstairs to scream into your pillow for thirty seconds, whatever it takes. Let it out before you get to the dance. Check yourself in the mirror after your little hissy fit because chances are your hair is a mess and/or your makeup is all Lady Marmaladed.

5 **Early on** in the date, arrange, and focus on, a time during the evening when you'll change. Suggest leaving the event early, changing into jeans and T-shirts or whatever, and being the first to hit the postprom parties. Having a light at the end of the tunnel is key to maintaining the perspective you'll need to survive.

6 **At the dance**, it is imperative that you do not disavow, disrespect, disappoint, or otherwise "dis" your date in any way, shape, or form. It's bad enough your date looks like crap; you don't need to draw even more attention to the problem with a big scene in front of your friends.

7 **Mingle**, mingle, and mingle some more. You may be tempted to encourage your date to slink around the perimeter of the gym (or "ballroom," if you insist . . .), but this behavior will only attract attention. Likewise, just "stopping by" at the prom, then immediately going MIA will also reek of disingenuousness, and people will think something much worse is going on. Instead, put yourself smack at the center of the action. With luck, witnesses will only barely notice your date. He/she will be but a small, if mildly noteworthy, piece in the crazy mélange that is prom.

8 **Have on hand** several ready-made responses for when your friends ask about the situation and stick to them (e.g., "What can I say? Can I have a sip of your punch?" or "Well, you know [insert offensive date's name here].") If you go into any more depth, you WILL be overheard. Decades of teen movies have proved this inevitability. Save your biting commentary for tomorrow, and even then limit it only to your nearest and dearest.

The bottom line: Remember, the last thing you want is a totally perfect prom. What you want is a memorable prom so that your prom stories, when you tell them to your college friends, future spouses, and/or grandchildren, generate laughs.

*All prom dates, no matter how good they look, seem a lot cheesier when you look back at prom night. No matter how good, or how bad, you and your date look for the prom, you'll cringe when you look back at the pictures. It's a fact of life.

#18 Unplanned, but Welcome, Affection

The problem: You get groped by your best friend's superhot BF/GF . . . and you like it.

The goal: To savor the moment while nullifying any chance of a repeat.

Before you begin: If the grope was an unwanted one, you're being sexually harassed and you need to take it seriously. Talk to someone who can help you (and you know who this is). However, if, and only if, you don't mind the grope AND if you have no regard for your best-friendship, understand that this is your best and only opportunity to take this forbidden nookie as far as you feel comfortable. If you take this route, prepare to live without your best friend, because he/she will find out and your friendship justifiably will be toast.

1 **Do the best** you can to absolve yourself of guilt. Remind yourself that this is not your fault. At least it wasn't at first.

2 **Shower** a couple of times. It's remarkable how clean your brain can feel when you thoroughly clean the outside.

3 **Make it clear** to the groper that no matter how well it worked out or how good it felt, you will never let it happen again. And mean it.

4 **Get hard evidence** if possible, and remind your groper that you could ruin his/her life if he/she discloses things. Sound like blackmail? It isn't, unless you need it to be. Consider it insurance.

5 **Do not**, under any circumstances, let it happen again. One incident is hard enough to cover up or deny. Two or more is impossible.

6 **Do not change** your day-to-day interaction with the groper. You want to present a façade of status quo to the rest of the world, and since you're in the same social circle, that means maintaining your relationships. If you overcompensate and appear to get closer to your groper, you'll arouse suspicion. If you suddenly start to hate and ignore the groper, you'll arouse even more. Maintain normal relations at all costs . . . no more, no less.

7 **Do not**, under any circumstances, volunteer the information to your best friend. No matter what those daytime talk shows suggest.

8 **Do not accept** or return follow-up phone calls, e-mails, pages, notes, or any other communication about the event from the groper. "Discussing" the situation will only make it bigger and potentially add to the drama,

because you'll both say things you don't really mean and you'll misunderstand each other and suddenly something that could have faded mercifully into your secret history becomes a big-ass deal. Don't be a sucker for this. Let it go, completely, now.

9 **If you get busted**, deny. You might get away with it. If you don't, you'll have to accept the consequences, which could be anything up to and including losing your friend, your groper, and your reputation. (See step #5.) Which would be the same punishment you'd receive if you told the truth. So you might as well try to deny.*

The bottom line: *Hooking up with a friend's make-out partner is a massive breach of the contract of friendship. If and when you get busted, you must accept and suffer through your punishment.*

*Note: Attempting to blame the grope-fest on your friend's significant other won't really work. Because, let's be serious, you participated. (Unless, of course, the grope was unwanted, in which case you should refer to the "Before you begin . . ." section.)

#19 Hostile Front Line

The problem: Your mother (and/or father) tells you to "stay the hell away" from that kid who you have a massive, complete, and all-encompassing crush on. Mom (and/or Dad) says your crush is a bad influence, and Mom (and/or Dad) doesn't like the look of him/her.

The goal:
To minimize parental interference in your social life.

Before you begin: Consider whether or not your mother (or father) has ample and appropriate reason to hate your crush so much. Be honest with yourself. And if she (or he) does have a good reason, suck it up and stay the hell away from the kid.

Keep your crush the hell away from your mom/dad. At all costs.

Never, ever admit that you are dating him/her. Parents frequently use the line, "Look, I already know you're seeing <u>(insert crush's name here)</u>. Let's talk about it." This is a trap.* They're probably bluffing.

3 **Have a rock-solid alibi** whenever you're seeing (insert crush's name here) or speaking on the phone. To be as safe as possible, arrange an alibi with a sibling and/or best friend every time you plan on seeing the crush.**

Bottom line: It's important to keep reevaluating this crush, just like any relationship, on its own terms. Don't decide you like your crush even more just because the 'rents can't stand him/her. And definitely don't hang on to him/her if you've lost that loving feeling, just because it's making some kind of statement to your parents. That would be so tragically Lifetime Movie Network.

*Note: Police and military interrogators also use this sneaky trick. Watch carefully.

**Note: The best possible arrangement is a mutual unlimited alibi agreement in which both parties agree to provide solid, pre-agreed-upon alibis for each other whenever needed. These can be agreements between two parties or three-way agreements. More than three parties involved in the same agreement is possible but discouraged because leaks are more likely with more participants.

#20 Pass-Around Patty (or Pat)

The problem: You bring your new BF/GF to a party, only to learn that he/she's been around a few blocks . . . according to more than a few of your friends, several of whom actually even hooked up with your new squeeze.

The goal: To stand tall and remain honorable.

Before you begin: Before you judge anyone's past, be sure to take a look at your own. It's not a crime to have dated a lot. However, not everyone will understand this, and face it: If you hook up with someone that a good number of your friends have "been" with, you're going to face some misunderstandings. And sometimes, they're going to be ill.

1   **Act like** you already knew. Practice, and use, the following: "No sh*t! Who cares?" If people think you know and think that you don't care, they'll drop it. (Or at least they'll just take to talking behind your back, which you can, and should, always choose to ignore.)

2   **Spend a respectable** amount of time at the party. Remind yourself that there is no shame unless you act ashamed.

3   **Cut the evening** slightly short to leave time for one-on-one discussion between you and your date. If he or she wants to discuss the situation, hear them out, not only because they'll need to talk it out, but because you'll be better informed if you get their side of the story.

4   **Figure out** which single source you trust the most and get more detailed information. Force your source away from speculation and/or gossip. Get facts, and only facts. Not because you'll use those facts to dis your new BF/GF, but because the facts are generally way less crazy than the scenarios your mind dreams up. If you get the hard facts, your brain will just stick to those, and chances are they're much tamer than the stories you heard.

5   **If your best source** is also your best friend and you have no reason to mistrust this person, take what they say seriously. For example, if they claim to have hooked up with your GF recently enough to make you uncomfortable, you might want to take a rain check on this relationship for now. Not to punish the new BF/GF, but because you'll need time to get the hell over it before you'll be able to give the relationship a good, honest shot.

6   **Do not show** any interest at all to your other friends. Your mission here is to appear mysteriously uninterested in the "revelations" on all fronts. Your best friends will admire your independence, which is a good place to be with your friends.*

7 **Get over it.** Begin to make decisions about this relationship based on what's going on in the relationship now. The past is the past, which is now over.

The bottom line: Remember, most past hookups get way exaggerated, and they rarely, if ever, represent a clear and present threat to your new relationship. Keep your eye on the ball that's in play, not on any games that are already over.

*Note: Some of your friends will adapt an "I told you so!" attitude if your new relationship doesn't work out. Suck it up, because they did.

#21 Indecent Proposals

The problem: That ex who still has a crush on you (even though you're so over it) shows up in the school parking lot right as class lets out, blaring love songs out of his/her car and proposing to you on one knee in front of everyone.

The goal: A graceful getaway.

Before you begin: However strong your instinct may be to loudly tell off your ex for this shameless ploy for your pity, and the pity of the school population at large, keep in mind that it took mad guts for your ex to act like such a freak, and he/she deserves some props for that. No matter how totally embarrassing it is for you. So be nice.

1   **If you're lucky** enough to find out about the situation early enough and you can slip out before anyone (up to and including your ex) finds out, do so.

2   **If escape** is impossible, concentrate on your breathing. You could be facing a rough few minutes, and although total panic might seem like a good option, it won't help. Breathe.

3   **Stay for** the entire performance. If you leave while he/she is still singing, you'll appear unkind, cold, heartless, or worse.

4   **After the performance**, approach your ex, thank him or her, and accept any flowers, food, or other perishable gifts. (To turn these down would simply be unkind.) Refuse jewelry, music, or other "hard" gifts, at least for the time being. Gifts like these often have the side effect of making you feel somehow obligated to your ex, which is not where you want to be.

5   **If you're more convinced** than ever that this is NOT the person for you, retreat with the ex (and a friend if possible) to a less public place (at the other end of the parking lot, in the hallway in school—someplace where the eyes of the student body aren't all fixed on you). There, reassert your position that you two are not suited for each other and leave.*

6   **Keep in mind** that many of your friends will consider this situation to be an "Awww . . ." moment, and they may make you think you should reconsider everything and get back together with your ex. Resist this, remembering that he/she is your ex for at least one very good reason. Right? (If not, take this opportunity to get back together. This is likely your last shot.)

The bottom line: *If your heart's been sufficiently melted, agree only to discuss things further. Do not agree to get back together or even to a date beyond the initial discussion. No matter how cute you find this display, remember your past together. It wasn't all that pretty, was it? Besides, the goal here, as you'll recall, is a graceful getaway, not a reconciliation. (See above.)*

*Usually the hardest part about dumping someone is having them hate you. Remind yourself that no matter how mean you're feeling right now, it'd be a lot meaner to stick around in a relationship you don't want to be a part of.

SOCIAL CRISES

Your social life is more precarious than you think it is. Why? Because everyone's laughing at you. (Not, as they'd like you to believe, merely near you.) Okay, maybe they're not. Maybe they're totally ignoring you. Either way, face it, your social life can seriously suck!

#22 You're Dating Who?

The problem: You can't stand your best friend's new boyfriend/girlfriend. It's not like you think he/she is seriously bad news or anything; it's just that he/she annoys the crap out of you with his/her bizarre social behavior, not to mention his/her fashion choices. You're embarrassed for your friend.

The goal: To make your point without dissing anyone too hard.

Before you begin: Thank your lucky stars that you're not the one dating this freak. That is, unless you really want to be dating him/her, and you're just jealous, which would explain why he/she annoys you so much in the first place.

1 **Tell your friend** how you feel. No holds barred. Follow up your assessment with something along the lines of ". . . but you know I love you." Do this one time, and one time only.

2 **When you get** the urge to complain about the BF/GF again, don't follow through. Even if he/she explicitly asks for your feedback, say, "You already know how I feel."

3 **Avoid the BF/GF** whenever possible. The more he/she's out of your sight, the more he/she's out of your mind.

4 **Depending** on the particular items that annoy you about the BF/GF, you may consider an intervention. Score some one-on-one time with the BF/GF (perhaps while your friend is running into the Circle K for a sixty-four-ounce diet cola) and drop the science: "Dude, the way you laugh, all high-pitched like that, is really annoying. And that socks-with-your-Birkenstocks thing? That's gotta go. Trust me." He/she may hate you, but you hate him/her, anyway, so who cares? You never know, he/she may even take your POV into consideration and change! (Caveat: In some cases, an intervention may make the BF/GF amp up the questionable behavior, but this, too, can work to your advantage, as the amp-up might hasten the end of the relationship.)

5 **Get over it.**

The bottom line: Unless he/she is seriously abusive or a criminal or something, this situation falls into the "none of your business" category.

#23 Drugstore Dilemma

The problem: You're in line at the drugstore with a basketful of embarrassing products, like tampons, Jolene body-hair bleach, foot odor powder, maybe some condoms, and a Fleet enema . . . and you run into the biggest crush you've ever had. Or the biggest enemy.

The goal: To minimize the impact of the evidence.

Before you begin: *Be certain to buy other items, preferably large, inexpensive, innocuous items (like paper towels) that can be used to cover and camouflage other items in your basket. You can always decide not to buy them at the checkout.*

Know the opposition: Take a good, hard look at what's in his/her basket. If his/her spread is equally gross, you're probably safe.

If you're lucky enough to see him/her before he/she sees you, bolt to a part of the store he/she would never need to visit and stay there.

(Consider the sanitary napkin or makeup sections if your challenger is a boy, the men's grooming section if it's a girl you're avoiding.)

3 **If you can** do so in a clandestine fashion, consider dropping your basket and heading to the magazine section. You can always restock after he/she is gone.

4 **Defuse the situation** by copping to it first. Say something like, "Do you know where they keep the Depends?" He/she will be flabbergasted and not know what to do.

5 **Consider a variation** on the following: "Check this out. I'm shopping for my mother. Can you believe how gross she is?" Work on your delivery in the car on the way to the drugstore, just in case.

6 **Do not giggle** nervously. This will only compound your embarrassment.

7 **Find a new drugstore** for the future, preferably one that's not in your own school district. Consider using the Internet for all future personal-care needs. Also, many drugstores and mega-retail stores stay open twenty-four-hours so consider shopping at strange times.

The bottom line: You know better than to be truly ashamed of normal hygiene issues. You know all this stuff is normal. But still, wouldn't it be a nicer universe if no one had to see you with a basketful of stuff whose ads you go, "Ew!" to every time they air?

#24 Unwanted Makeover

The problem: It's the annual prom fund-raiser again, and this year you and the committee are auctioning off a full makeover—to be completed then and there at the event. Little did you know that the whole committee pitched in and bought the prize for you, and you're now being hauled off for a quickie makeover.

The goals: To endure, to be game, and to cull as much professional advice as you can.

Before you begin: Understand that your "friends" did this not because they think you're really U-G-L-Y, but because they probably just want to embarrass the bejesus out of you. Nothing more, nothing less. However, the fact is you're getting a free makeover, and how often does that happen? Take advantage of the opportunity.

1. **Give yourself** a reality check: You do, in fact, need a makeover. Everyone does.

2. **Understand** also that you will have a chance to get them back eventually. Worry about that later. In the meantime, you're here now, so you might as well come out the other end looking great.

75

3 **Wrestle** the fear and pessimism out of your brain and keep an open mind. After all, you're going to be shown off to the crowd when this is over, and no one looks good with a big ol' scowl on their face. You might as well come across as a good sport instead of a total buzzkill.

4 **Don't be shy** about asking for another outfit choice if what they initially select isn't really you. Refer to "Before you begin" above, and remember, these professionals are at your disposal for a limited amount of time. Appeal to their sense of perfectionism, encourage them to do their best work, ever, on you.

5 **Be honest** about your sizes when they ask. It's one thing to try on a pair of size zero jeans in a dressing room; it's another to do it in front of a crowd. Tell the truth.

6 **Keep smiling**, even if you're horrified at the result. Repeat: "I can shower and change as soon as I get home" as often as necessary to make yourself believe it.

7 **Brace yourself** for your picture to appear in the yearbook, because it will.

The bottom line: The best thing about a public makeover is that it'll be over soon. Just ask anyone who's ever appeared on Fashion Emergency!

#25 Public Rejection

The problem: You ask out your crush, and he or she laughs. In your face. Then he or she tells everyone, and they laugh. Before you know it, you're this close to being laughed out of school.

The goal: To restore self-confidence.

Before you begin: Pat yourself on the back for being brave enough to pop the question in the first place. That took some serious guts on your part. Props. Now slap yourself upside the head. What were you thinking? Seriously. Your crush laughed at you! (There. You've got that out. It was inevitable.)

1 **Shore up** an alliance with your best friend. He/she will be required to provide you with unlimited shoulder-crying and kick-boxing time as you relieve yourself of the tension that inevitably comes with public humiliation.

2 **Practice the following** comment for use when people bring up the situation with you, which they will.* "What?" Say it indignantly. Also try "Yeah, so what?" or even "What the hell do you care?" (Feel free to use a Brooklyn accent, even if you're from Tulsa or Orlando. It's just more effective that way.)

3 **Laugh louder** than your crush. After all, it's your word against his/hers, and even if no one believes you, hey . . . at least you tried.

4 **Promise yourself** that you will never, ever ask this person out again, under any circumstances, ever, anywhere. Dude, he/she laughed at you! That's harsh.

5 **Promise yourself**, also, that if he/she ever comes around and asks you out, you will say no, unequivocally and loudly. No matter how bad you think you want to say yes. I mean come ON, he/she laughed at you! So uncool.

The bottom line: The best thing you can do for yourself now is to get back in the game as soon as possible. There are other crushes to ask out, and the sooner you score a victory in the game of love, however small, the faster your pride will find itself on the path to restoration.

***Whether they appear** to be sympathetic or hostile, they want the same thing: the dirty details so they can feel somehow superior to you.

#26 Dream Theft

The problem: You and your best friend (the one who's determined to become a movie star) audition for the same leading role in your school play, and even though you didn't really want the role all that bad (well, okay, secretly you did . . .), you get picked. And he/she's pissed as hell.

The goal: To adjust to life as a diva while doing your best (really) to preserve the friendship.*

Before you begin: Congratulations!

Thank your friend for going through the audition process with you. Sympathize with him/her. Try to do this without being condescending, and don't linger on this step.

Do not apologize. It's not your fault you got picked, and by apologizing, it almost makes it sound like you had something to do with it, when really it's the director who recognized you as the genius entertainer you are, so if your friend is gonna be mad at anybody, they should get mad at the director. Besides, isn't he/she your friend? Shouldn't he/she be happy for you?

Do not, under any circumstances whatsoever, give up your role, hoping that it'll save your friendship. It might feel like a bighearted thing to do, but in all honesty, it's just dumb. And it won't work. Don't do it.

Dive in. You've got a role to play, you've got a lot of work to do, and you should be psyched. (Sweet!) And you can't help it if it shows. But do not flaunt it in his/her face. Just because you're best friends (or were best friends) doesn't mean he/she is about to help you with your lines. You're probably better off doing that kind of stuff with other people for now. He/she still resents you.

Tread lightly if he/she decides to accept a smaller role in the same production. If he/she sticks around, he/she may resent you, and you may end up hating each other even more. There may be more passive-aggressive action than you can be expected to stomach. Not to mention that you run the risk of being sabotaged onstage by a disgruntled best friend. (And we all know what disgruntlement can lead to.)

Help him/her find another activity to get lost in. Since you're acting, maybe he/she could sing. Or take pottery lessons. Or clean the elephant cage at the zoo. Like you care. Oh, what the hell, get him/her to audition for a role in a production several miles away. Even if you know they suck onstage. Once they've become distracted, they'll pretend they hated this whole acting thing from the beginning.

The bottom line: Don't spend too much time trying to smooth things over when really, you did nothing that should require smoothing over. Besides, you should be too busy for this. Focus your energies on your role, and nail it on opening night. The last thing you need is a bloodsucking ex-best friend getting in the way of your debut. Go learn your lines!

Note: This advice only applies if you really wanted the part in the first place. If you don't actually want the part and also actually like your friend, turn the part down with riveting, dramatic reluctance.

#27 Yak Attack

The problem: You're partying with your crew, and you agree to a drink "just this once" and end up wasted. And you've gotta call one of your parents for a ride home. You blame it on lost keys, and they never suspect a thing until you hurl in the car.

The goal: To deal with the inevitable punishment. (There's no way you're getting out of it.)

Before you begin: First of all, no matter what it feels like at the moment, you did, in fact, do the right thing by calling them instead of driving yourself home. This is a fact, no matter how much your life feels like it sucks right now.

1 **Attempt a denial**, no matter how pathetic. "I must have food poisoning or something" might sound lame, but you've got nothing to lose.

2 **Ask**, or even beg if necessary, to table the inevitable "conversation" until the following morning, when you're less likely to say something really stupid.

3 **Under no circumstances** should you make a play for sympathy at this time or the next morning. While there is no embarrassment like drinking too much and acting like a schmo, and no pain like a hangover, your parents

have been there before, and they'll show you precious little sympathy along the way. They'll see your current condition as an appropriate, cosmic punishment for your overindulgent actions.

4 **When the conversation** finally happens, meekly and humbly remind your parents that you made one responsible choice during the evening: You called them instead of driving home.

5 **Don't say anything** to your parents that sounds like, "Gimme a break! Didn't you get into trouble with booze when you were my age?" Parents never, ever appreciate this because it just makes them feel old.

6 **Promise**, profusely and repeatedly, that you'll clean up the car.

7 **Thoroughly clean** up the car. And then take it to a professional. Don't attempt to do the entire job yourself because it will not work. Take it to one of those places where they shampoo the carpet and everything for you, and pay whatever it takes. It's a known fact that there is no whiff known to humankind quite as noxious or long-lingering as stale vomit, and you simply don't have the knowledge or means to deal with it yourself.

8 **Accept your punishment**, whatever it may be, willingly and without protest. There's a good chance you'll be paying for this misstep for the entire foreseeable future.

The bottom line: You really did do the right thing by getting a ride from the 'rents. Really.

#28 Misdressed and Misunderstood

The problem: You put together a fantastic Carmen Miranda/Zorro costume for the Halloween party. You're at the front door before you realize it's not a costume party.

The goal: To regain some dignity.

Before you begin: This is a defining moment in your life. How you act now, tonight, will determine how others react to you tonight, and it will be so memorable no matter what happens that those actions and reactions could make a massive difference in your near and distant future. Shine, and your future will shine. Cave, and your future will be bleak.

1. **Get yourself** some punch.

2. **Party down!**

The bottom line: When you make this kind of faux pas, there's no escaping it. Your challenge is, then, to own what you've done and work it. It's a great life-lesson situation, and if you can project confidence even through a fashion crisis, you'll carry the victory with you for the rest of your life.

#29 Doppelganger Blues

The problem: Someone you know well cops your entire look.

The goal: To preserve your (solo) place on the fashion ladder . . . and to get over yourself.

Before you begin: Remind yourself, as often as necessary, that imitation is, in fact, the sincerest form of flattery. It's a cliché for a reason.

1. **Grit your teeth** and say, "You look great." Don't get nasty. It will only make you look desperate and immature, which you are if you really let this kind of thing get to you. Besides, if you're truly the great fashion mind you consider yourself to be, you can handle this, and any other, style challenge. Right?

2. **Dig into** your closet and yank out some of those You Classics you haven't seen in a while. Rock these originals while plotting and assembling a new look. Stick with totally unique pieces that no one else has, you know, the ones you love, and mix those with superbasic jeans and T-shirts. This will get you through the transition phase.

The bottom line: You don't 'own' style. And besides, styles are for changing. Take this as a message, a perfect opportunity to shake up your own look. You're the trendsetter, so set a new trend already.

LEGAL DRAMA

Not to make light of a serious situation, but we will. (Note, however, that there is some sound advice in here. Don't mess with the law.)

#30 Warranted, If Unplanned-for, Arrest

The problem: You attend a World Bank/human rights protest (notwithstanding the fact that you have no clue what the issues involved are) in hopes of catching the eye of the hottest activist in school. To prove your conviction to the cause (and get a date), you even trespass on restricted government property. That's when you get arrested.

The goal: To follow the rules.

Before you begin: Okay, so you've found yourself on the rough side of the law. At this point it no longer matters why you're being taken into custody. What matters now is that the cops are in charge and you are not. Respecting this is critical to your well-being and that of your future.

DO NOT RESIST ARREST, UNDER ANY CIRCUMSTANCES. Cooperate. If you've done nothing illegal or if you've committed only the most minor of infractions, you'll be free to go soon enough. But when or how you leave police custody is not your decision. If you try to run, or take a swing at the arresting officer, or otherwise attempt to interfere, you'll have committed a much more serious offense, one that will certainly prejudice the system against you. Do not insult, threaten, or talk back to any officials. Keep your head down and your mouth shut.

(Note: Experienced protesters will often go limp and make the cops carry them out of the situation. This technique is only for the pros and is only effective when there are abundant news media present.)

If you're carrying anything illegal, like a joint or a weapon, do not try and ditch it. Turn it over. Again, cooperating will only help you.

If handcuffed, relax your hands. Clenching your fists and/or twisting your wrists can cause extensive superficial wounds, from cuts to bruises. They've got you. Relax.

Ignore the chaos going on around you. Focus on what the police tell you to do, and behave. Postpone emotional breakdowns, reputation freak-outs, and bad-hair maintenance indefinitely.

Avoid all face contact with all photographers, video crews, and the like. You do not want to end up on the evening news or, worse, *Cops*, under any circumstances. No matter how hot your outfit is. You will not get discovered that way, and Grandma shouldn't have to explain your behavior to her mahjong partners. (You know they watch *Cops*, don't you?)

6   **Answer no questions** shouted by reporters. They will misquote you. Again, avoid notoriety at all costs.

7   **Always be polite.** Again, do not insult, threaten, or talk back to any officials.

8   **At the station**, do not talk unless you absolutely must. Do not admit that you've done anything wrong. Comply with all orders they give you, but remember: You have the right to remain silent, at least for the time being. (See "Your Rights," next page.) Keeping quiet is much smarter than trying to come up with excuses. (Your parents might not have heard them all yet, but the cops have. Guaranteed.) "Talking your way out of it" is impossible at this stage. Do not attempt.

9   **Use your one** phone call wisely. This means calling a parent. If you're underage, a parent is the only one who can spring you. (Note: "Underage" means different things in different jurisdictions, but under eighteen is generally considered "underage.") Besides, the 'rents will find out, anyway. You may get grounded forever, but at least you won't be in jail all night. Do not squander your one phone call on your boyfriend. He's probably too drunk to drive, anyway. Do not call a friend because it'll be all over school by Monday. Call a parent, period.

10 **If your family** can't hook you up with a lawyer, accept the public defender the authorities provide you with. Be honest with them. Believe it or not, they aren't on anyone's side. Yet.

Your Rights

Remember, these really are your rights, not just some lines from a TV show:

You have the right to remain silent.

This means that you don't have to say a word. At least not yet.

Anything you say can and will be used against you.

This means that whatever comes out of your mouth counts. Cops hear and take note of everything you say, and if they're ever called as witnesses in your case, the courts will likely believe what they say. Don't say anything you don't mean, even in the heat of the moment. In other words, don't say anything. Just to be safe.

You have the right to speak to an attorney and to have an attorney present during any questioning.

This means that you get to run everything by a lawyer before saying anything. And that lawyer knows better than you do what you should and/or shouldn't do or say. Face it, you don't know jack about the criminal justice system. Get a lawyer.

If you cannot afford an attorney, one will be provided for you at government expense.

This means that if you don't have the cash for a lawyer (and don't want to come up with it), they'll hook you up with a free one. These lawyers, called public defenders or public advocates, are paid by the state to take on cases like yours. In most cities and counties, this will assure you of competent legal assistance (although in recent years public advocates have come under fire in some counties for inadequate representation). At best, a public defender will be a great help; at worst, it's probably better than nothing. Accept the freebie—unless you have your own.

#31 Winona Forever

The problem: You're at the mall, trying to decide between the new Jay-Z CD and the new Linkin Park, knowing that you can't afford both, and before you know it, you've been caught "accidentally" shoplifting.

The goal: To pay up and move on.

Before you begin: Don't shoplift. Sure, you might get away with it, but you might not, and let's be real: You don't want to get caught shoplifting. How would you ever explain that one to your crush?

Thank your lucky stars that this is a misdemeanor and chances are you'll get off with probation or community service or a fine.

Give it back, whatever it was, as quickly and quietly as possible. You don't want the cops involved, and you might get out of it if you're cool about it.

If the cops do get involved, don't try to explain yourself. This might be a good time to speak with an attorney. Even if it was truly accidental, it was definitely stupid enough to warrant punishment. Whether you meant to or not, you removed the stuff from the store without paying, and that's a smackdownable offense.

4   **Apologize** to your family and mean it. After all, you not only embarrassed the hell out of yourself, you have embarrassed the hell out of your entire family. Apologize, then promise that you'll never do it again, and mean it.

5   **Don't tell** anyone you don't need to tell. It will be misconstrued as bragging, and you don't want to be known for bragging about committing a crime.

6   **Get a job**, or another job, or yet another job as soon as possible. Make sure you have enough cash to buy—instead of steal—what you need.

7   **See a counselor** or shrink. Some people have a real, honest mental and/or emotional disorder that causes them to lift stuff even when they don't need it. If you think you're one of those people, you can get the help you need. I suggest you do it before really blowing it.

8   **Never, ever**, ever do it again. Ever. Seriously.

> **The bottom line:** Don't shoplift, even by accident. You really don't need to at all, and let's face it, getting caught shoplifting has to be one of the most embarrassing, humiliating, totally unnecessary things that can happen to you.

#32 Quick Cash

The problem: Your friend gets arrested and needs bail.

The goal: To get out of it.

Before you begin: *Ignore whatever it is that got your friend in jail in the first place. Not only do you not have the cash for this kind of thing (even if you do), you definitely don't want to get mixed up in anything he/she is involved in. I mean, don't you ever watch* Court TV? *That could be you. No good.*

1. **Don't give** him/her money. Refer him/her to his/her family and/or other responsible adult.

2. **See step #1.**

The bottom line: *Don't worry. He/she will find a way to get the cash. You and your bank account are not available for bail.*

SCHOOL BLOWS

As if school weren't bad enough, what with the homework and labs and studying and tests and all, there's also the fact that school hallways are the venue of choice for full-on social, emotional, and physical embarrassment. More lifelong traumas are made in school hallways than almost anywhere else on the planet.

Ready?

#33 Summer Sentence

The problem: You blew off your homework, or finals, or both, or whatever, and now you have to sit your way through an entire season of summer school!

The goal: To take care of business—on the way, way down-low.

Before you begin: Do it. No matter how humiliating it is, no matter how much you don't think you belong in summer school, no matter how much you don't think you deserve to repeat a year, the fact is you blew it somewhere along the line, and now you gotta pay. So pay up.

Lobby your school and your parents to let you go to a different school to attend class and fulfill your requirements. Preferably one far, far across town. You want no one in your class who knows you and no one who ever will. You have enough on your plate with having homework during July; you don't need the headaches all the explaining will lead to.

Keep your head down. You want no one in your class to even notice you. Who knows who else from your school has already read this book and switched across town, just like your sly self?

If you're facing summer school, feel free to tell everyone you're "working" all summer. After all, that's kinda true. Kinda. And besides, situations like these are what white lies are all about.

The bottom line: For Pete's sake, nail it this time around. Do every single assignment as well as every piece of extra credit. Show up every single day. Be polite to your teacher. Ask for extra help if you need to. In short, suck it up and play by the rules. This is your big chance to never, ever have to do anything like this again. Keep ending up in summer school and the rest of your life will totally bite. This is not a threat—it's a fact.

CHICK'N HUT
Welcome Freshmen 10% OFF with Student I.D.
BACK TO SCHOOL 5 piece DINNER

#34 Future Shock

Before you begin: To avoid this situation in the first place, have a good relationship with your college adviser. If he/she is any good, you're bound to get in somewhere. After all, their job is on the line. If you don't have a college adviser at your school, ask your guidance counselor. Tip: Be really nice to whoever you ask for help. He/she will help you if he/she likes you. But if not, you could be up a creek.

Make an immediate appointment with your school's guidance counselor or college adviser, if you have one.

Hit the college section at your local megabookstore. You haven't missed every single deadline quite yet. Some colleges, especially state and municipal schools, take applications right up until just days before classes actually begin.

3 **Don't give up.** Begin beefing things up and making yourself a more attractive candidate. Even though you didn't get in this time around, chances are there are plenty of application deadlines you haven't missed yet, and there's always next year. Plus you may start at a less attractive school and transfer up. Who knows? The fact is you weren't the student they were looking for, so you need to make some changes to sweeten up your applications.

a. Check your test scores. If they weren't high enough, get a job (or ask your parents for cash) and buy yourself a test-prep course. Then attend it and pay attention. They'll do whatever it takes to get your scores up . . . after all, it's just as embarrassing for them if they don't succeed.

b. Check the rest of your application. If you think you're missing some classes they wanted you to take, sign up and take similar classes somewhere in town.

c. Check the list of places you applied. If you aimed too high, be sure to include some "safety" schools next time around, just in case.

4 **Consider taking** the year or semester off and reapplying later. (Note: This does NOT mean you get to sit on your ass for the next several months watching DirectTV and hoping you'll get into the same places that rejected you first time around. This means you gotta fill that time with something that will make you a hell of a lot more attractive to those institutions. Like scoring a cool internship, or volunteering full-time at a local Red Cross or Habitat for Humanity, or taking classes at a local community college that accepts anyone who can pay, or, if you have the cash, traveling around the world. Or something.

The fact is, if you take this year off, you need to really do something with it. Like I said before, you need to fatten yourself up for the college market.)

5   **Submit** an application to the Tastee-Freez and start practicing your soft-serve technique. It's gonna be a long life. Oh, just kidding. Gimme a break and laugh at yourself already.

> *The bottom line:* This truly is not the end of the world as you know it. Don't believe the hype and sell your future short now. Amp things up for the next round, which you will be participating in. Got that?

#35 Choke-a-delic

The problem: You break the rules to go off campus for lunch, and your friend starts to choke on her Nachos Belle Grande.

The solution:
To save a life.

> *Before you begin: Check your head, and don't try to be a hero. This is no time to show off, it's a time to get any help you can. Even if you know what to do in this situation, try to find help.*

1 **Don't panic.** (Yeah, right.)

2 **If you're** in the car, pull over and flag someone down to help. Pronto.

3 **Yell for help**, even if you know what to do. There's a good chance that someone at the restaurant knows even better what to do. Make sure every single person in the entire restaurant knows what's going on. So what if you're embarrassed to draw attention to yourself? Dude, your friend is choking!

4 **Look around** for that What to Do If Someone Is Choking poster every restaurant is legally required to have up, even skanky fast-food places. (In fact, you should have read this and figured it out already. In fact, next

time you're in a restaurant, look for it and read it. In fact, memorize it. And in fact, tell all your friends to do the same. Seriously. You could be the next one choking, and it would suck if your loser friends had no freakin' idea what the hell to do.) Follow the directions.

5 **Believe it or not**, even if you can't get yourself off the hook for being off campus, don't think twice about getting help from your school if you need it. Seriously, suck on a little detention to save your friend's life. You'd expect nothing less from him/her, right? (Note: Same goes if you've got a friend who you think is in danger of overdosing or getting alcohol poisoning or something. There's a point where you need to reality-check yourself back onto the planet and worry about the repercussions later, after everyone's safe and taken care of.)

6 **Don't order** another taco. Lunch is SO over. Get back to class, ya dip.

The bottom line: It's well worth looking into first-aid courses in your area. Check with the local Red Cross or firehouses or hospitals in your 'hood. Chances are they offer something. They'll teach you everything from the Heimlich to CPR. It's good to know, you might get to practically make out with strangers, and you'll never have to worry about not knowing what to do in an emergency again.

#36 Hoop Nightmares

The problem: There's one second left on the clock, the score is tied 44–44, and you've just been fouled by the defending team at the national championships. Your free throw will decide the outcome. Too bad you waffle both shots, costing your team the whole tournament.

The goal: To be a loser with at least a shred of dignity.

Before you begin: You're an athlete, so you know you're going to beat yourself up about this pretty badly. So start giving yourself a break now, because it'll be a while before it takes effect.

Immediately after missing the basket, run off the court in tears, even if you're a six-foot-five bruiser with tattoos and an attitude. Just kidding. Don't ever do that.

Do not speak to anyone in the locker room, especially that annoying girl from the school newspaper who wants to write a "sympathetic" article about you. She's lying. Be polite enough to say, "No, thanks," or "Excuse me," but keep your head down and don't invite any attention. (Note: This also means: Don't throw a tantrum.)

Believe it or not, people really aren't mad at you, they're just deflated after losing a really important game. If the whole team was better, you wouldn't have been in the position to make a do-or-die point like that. But don't bring this up quite yet. It's just not safe.

Likewise, don't start asking for forgiveness or anything like that. The instant you do, it's totally like admitting that it was all your fault.

When you return to school, take the ribbing and admit that it sucks to be you.

Commit to joining the team next year, unless you're graduating. The last thing you want to do is stay in high school just to play ball. Now that would be the mark of a real loser.

The bottom line: Believe it or not, screwing things up this severely can actually be good for your social life, if you play your cards right. Generous, gracious losers are considered charming and adorable by many a member of the opposite (and same) sex.

#37 You Got Nothin'

The problem: All you've heard about all semester is how the only grade that matters in your physics class is the grade you get on your huge final research paper/project. You've known the due date since the beginning of the semester, and all the teacher can talk about is how he will accept no papers whatsoever after the due date. It's like he's trying to make a point or something. Anyway, it was due today, so how could you possibly have spaced it?

The goal: To avoid a zero.

Before you begin: *Teachers often have barks worse than their bites, and there's usually a way around "no-exception" rules like this one. However, if you want to find the loopholes, you have to kiss some serious butt. And it may take a while. Oh, and another thing: This will work if, and only if, you are generally a good student. If you're lousy most of the time, you can forget it.*

1 **Ask your teacher** to let you turn it in tomorrow.

2 **Beg your teacher** to let you turn it in tomorrow.

3 **Attempt to strike** a deal with your teacher. Offer to accept points off for lateness.

4 **Offer your teacher** a bribe.*

5 **Promise** to do piles of extra credit.

6 **Cry.** (Even though none of the steps I have yet listed will likely work, it's important to go through as many of them as you can stomach to vividly illustrate to your teacher how much this means to you, and to feed his/her ego.)

7 **If you still** end up with a zero, cozy up to the fact that you're going to have to repeat the class. That could mean summer school, doubling up next semester, taking a night class, or (shudder) postponing graduation.

The bottom line: Do whatever it takes to deal with this. Send your pride packing and suck up hard. Better to humiliate yourself now than have to live with a wasted semester.

When bribing your teacher, stick to money. It won't work, but the right eyes might see it as charming or even comedic. You can certainly laugh it off easily enough. Do not offer any *special* favors; this will only make everyone uncomfortable and make you seem desperate and/or pathetic, and it will hurt your chances.

#38 Party Hearty

The problem: As president of the Key Club, you plan a huge blowout at the school to benefit your local animal shelter. You've been selling tickets for two weeks, and so far a whopping nine have been sold—all to members of the Mullet Appreciation Society. No one knows how bad things are except you, and the dance is only three days away.

The goals: To guarantee a massive turnout and protect your social life.

Before you begin: Don't waste time overthinking some huge, complicated gimmick to attract attendees. The best ways to get people in the door are almost always the most obvious: Good music and a hot crowd. Don't go chasing waterfalls.

1 **Up the DJ** quality. To hell with the school's "best" DJ; call around to nightclubs in town and beg a local pro to donate his/her time for a couple of hours to work the turntables. Tell 'em it's for the cute li'l puppies and kitties, and they'll totally do it.

2 **Likewise,** see if you can get a rocking local band to donate a half-hour set or something. Beg, plead, and be extremely persistent. Go for big names, small names. You never know. Musicians are always doing random benefits. It's considered cool. Plus they might attract the press, which could get you in the papers, which is the mark of a true partier.

3 **Spread the rumor** that Lance from *NSYNC is going to emcee.

4 **Notify people** that the official dress code is "dress to hook up."

5 **Convince** the guys' swim team (go through the principal or someone who can tell them that they have to) to raffle themselves off in their boxer shorts. The guys will draw the female crowd, which will in turn draw the male crowd, and you'll have a hit function on your hands.*

The bottom line: *It's not just about the kitties and puppies, it's about whether you'll have a social life after throwing a party no one came to. If it takes three days spent entirely on the phone, so be it. Next time you'll plan ahead, using these steps not as last resorts, but as springboards to ideas you'll implement well before the next party.*

*Note: Some school political organization or other will probably threaten to boycott the dance because you're peddling flesh, even though it's for a good cause. Don't worry. In fact, be psyched. This will dramatically increase ticket sales.

#39 Wearing the Loser Cap, Stylishly

The problem: You run for student council president . . . and come in last.

The goal: To deny you ever wanted to win in the first place.

Before you begin: Remind yourself, no matter how humiliated you feel, that you weren't running for your own ego, anyway. You were running to serve the public. So losing doesn't mean you're a loser, it means the voters are. (If you can convince yourself of this, feel free to skip the rest of the steps.)

When the results are announced, show no emotion whatsoever. Anything you do, from laughing to congratulating your opponent, could be misconstrued as sour grapes, which you don't want to be accused of being.

Practice the following comments, and use them until you've convinced everyone, including yourself, that they're true:

a. "I didn't even vote for myself!"

b. "My dad made me run for my college applications."

c. "I was totally on this medication that made me think I actually wanted to be on student council! Thank God I'm cured!"

d. "I totally won, but I decided to give the election to (winner's name here) because he/she needs it more than I do."

e. "(Winner's name here) totally cheated!"

f. "Like the student council president even matters, anyway!"

g. "You seriously think I wanted to be president? Are you insane? Someone must have put my name on the ballot. I had no clue!"

Never, ever run for any office again—unless you're certain you can win. Then again, weren't you pretty sure you'd win this time around?

The bottom line: To avoid this situation in the first place, don't run for office. There's really no reason to, anyway. You can certainly find more interesting ways to pad your college apps.

#40 For Boys Only: Unexpected Chubbies

The problem: You're giving a presentation to the entire class on the finer points of photosynthesis when that one new girl in the front row readjusts her bra strap and you suddenly sprout wood.

The goal: To deflate the situation.

Before you begin: First and foremost, do not panic. Stay cool. Keep in mind that no one in the room is really paying attention to you, anyway . . . so long as you keep from acting like a freak.

1 **Do not lose** your train of thought, and continue your presentation. No matter how arousing the view, focusing on photosynthesis might just be enough to bring you back to earth.

2 **Your first instinct** will be to clench your "special" muscles. Don't. Flexing below will only increase turgidity. Resist and relax. (Note: In the case of a partial chubby, resisting the urge to flex may actually speed deflation.)

3 **If you blush**, begin to laugh immediately. You cannot stifle a blush, but it's easy enough to explain away a giggle. ("Nothing, nothing. I just thought of something funny. No, it's okay, I don't want to share it with the class. Really, I don't.")

4 **Your best line** of defense is to hide. Scan for something large and opaque between you and your audience. Look for a desk, a chair, a file cabinet, or a trusted friend and move toward it, slowly and casually, but firmly. If there is no cover apparent, quickly turn and face the chalkboard—without losing track of your speech (see step #1). (Note: As you secure coverage, remember that you may have to choose who'll get a view and who won't. Prioritize realistically. Your teacher might get a chuckle, but she won't call you out. Your ex-girlfriend will spread it all over school. Your posse will point and bark. Choose your teacher.)

5 **Once you've obscured** the danger zone, you may want to attempt the three-point tuck (see next page). This technique is worth practicing whenever possible. In private, please.

6 **If cover** is scarce and/or unavailable, the next-best bet for a solidly pitched tent is to sit. This position creates a large wrinkle in baggier pants, which can house even the grandest of objects. The goal is not to tuck away, but to aim everything in the correct direction (depending on degree of rigidity, this could be up or to your preferred side) and let the heavy lifting happen as you sit. Success with this technique requires quite a bit of pelvic dexterity, and a little luck, and is also worth practicing at home. Again, in private. This cannot be stressed enough.

The bottom line: Know your options and know how to use them. Research might show that simply being prepared for any rising situation and aware that it could happen at any time can actually reduce the number of unplanned incidents. Then again, it might increase them. In any event, it's good to know what to do.

Stopping Stiff Situations Before They Start

To guarantee chubby-coverage in public, it's important to know your wardrobe. You'll find that some items are more conducive to camouflage than others. As a general rule, tighty-whiteys can help keep renegade appendages closer to home, while boxers are more likely to free willy.

However, many variables apply, from humidity, to fabric strength, to body shape, to sheer size and volume. Ample experimentation with many possible combinations of under- and outer garments will ensure optimum preparedness.

At least one female interviewed for this book pointed out that khaki-bound woodies are much more obvious than ones concealed by good, stiff jeans. Consider this when back-to-school shopping.

The Three-Point Tuck

The goal with this deft move is to make it look as natural as possible. Bend at the knees and move your hips to the side and back, creating slack in your jeans. At the same time, use your arm or the back of your hand to gently but firmly guide the unwelcome visitor upward. Its final position should be tucked snugly against your lower belly. Do not attempt to employ your waistband to hold things in place unless you're an expert. This frequently backfires.

ON-LINE HUMILIATION

You thought you were immune from humiliation when you were chatting on-line, didn't you? Well, forget it, because the best thing about humiliation is that it can, and will, follow you anywhere. And virtual humiliation is just as damaging as the kind you face in the real world.

#41 E-mail Mayhem

The problem: You accidentally push "send" on that e-mail you really didn't want to send at all. You know, the one where you confess your total love for your best friend's significant other.

The goal: Damage control.

Before you begin: This is the kind of situation that makes the mind race wildly out of control. You start worrying about how they'll respond and who they'll tell and everything, and you lose focus. Don't fall into this trap. With a little luck and some swift moves, you may be able to save yourself.

1 **Check your out box** immediately and delete anything that's in there. Some programs hold on to your mail for a couple of minutes before releasing it.

2 **If you're using** America Online, you can actually "unsend" e-mails that you've already sent. Other providers may have a similar recall feature. Use it.

3 **Unplug your modem**, if you're using one, quick. This'll only work if there's a glitch in your connection, anyway, but at this point, you need to

exploit everything you can think of, including potential weaknesses in your own system.

4 **Call the person** you're sending the e-mail to and hope you get them before they open it. Use the following: "Hey, what's up? Listen, I just want to apologize . . . I accidentally sent this e-mail to you that was really meant for someone else, not you, even though it says your name on it . . ." You can't expect them to buy it, but it's worth a shot just in case. They may go so far as to act like they buy it, which is good enough for the time being.

5 **In the future**, compose all e-mails on a word-processing program like Microsoft Word or Simple Text or something. Then, after thoroughly reading, rereading, editing, and revising the letter, copy and paste it into your e-mail program before sending.

The bottom line: Don't even come anywhere near saying something on-line that you wouldn't say in person. See, on-line communication is not something to hide behind . . . it only gives everyone else in the world a complete, written record of exactly what you said. In other words, it's way, way harder to take back an e-mail than it is to take back something you said out loud. And way, way easier to get busted.

#42 Haters.com

The problem: You're cruising around on-line when you come across an anti-you Web page.*

The goal: To rise above.

Before you begin: Pat yourself on the back. As any savvy Net celebrity knows, you're nuthin' until someone posts a Web page that's all about how much they hate you. Congratulations: You've arrived.

1 **Don't fight back.** The key to winning this war is to not take the bait. Do not engage. If you give in to anger, you will lose.

2 **Look it over** carefully. Check every single link. You want to know exactly what's being said. Check the site every day. (Don't listen to people who tell you to ignore it.)

3 **Write** a thank-you e-mail to the Webmaster. Nothing ticks off a potential enemy more than when you thank them. They did this to piss you off; if it has the opposite effect, that's called a backfire. Psych!

4 **Post** really horrible things about yourself if there's a bulletin board. If you can make them heinous enough, like you eat children, then no one will believe them, and by extension, they won't believe a damn thing on the whole site.

5 **Do not attempt** to hack in and alter the site. No matter how offensive it is, hacking that way is not only illegal, it's so illegal, you'll have the FBI at your door before you even log off. Which you do not want, under any circumstances. Believe me.

6 **If people ask** you about the site, tell them you think it's hilarious. Any other reaction, like it annoys you or pisses you off, could potentially give your haters more fuel for their fire.

The bottom line: Sure, it's painful, but who knows where this could lead? Cross your fingers and hope it turns into a Webwide campaign.

*Note: With anti-you Web sites, as with any kind of obsession someone has about you, there's a fine line between good satire and something truly threatening. If the Web site contains any threats directed at you or anyone else, even if they seem silly, call the cops. Seriously. 'Cause that isn't funny.

#43 Snoop Dog

The problem: You read your BF/GF's e-mail, and there's plenty of proof in there that he/she is totally cheating on you.

The goal:
To cover your ass while smacking down his/hers.

Before you begin: Do what you can as soon as possible to smooth this situation out as much as you can, but leave yourself ample time afterward to administer a thorough and complete smackdown upon yourself.

Do not read anyone else's e-mail, ever. Not only is it illegal, it's annoying as hell, even if you were doing it innocently, like as a little prank or to leave him/her a cute little note from him/herself or something. Don't do it.

If you were dumb enough to open someone else's e-mail, hack back in and reflag the "read" messages as "unread," if possible.

Understand that you are both guilty of ill acts of dishonesty. Your BF/GF shouldn't be cheating on you, but there's no excuse for you to be snooping that way. Y'all are both busted, both guilty of major, trust-breaking crimes against your relationship.

 The most honorable thing to do, at this point, would be to confess and disclose everything, and break up for a while so you can both reevaluate the situation and each other. Yeah, right. Like that ever happens except on the Oprah show.

Start talking with, and listening to, your BF/GF. If you two were communicating better, you wouldn't be needing to hack into his/her e-mail for the 411. Keep your eyes and ears open for a legitimate opportunity to raise the issue. That way you'll get his/her side of the story, and you'll be able to figure out the whole truth (which might or might not be what you thought it was . . .) and make a decision about what to do.

Learn your lesson, and don't ever do it again.

> **The bottom line:** If you find yourself in this situation in the first place, the chances are you have a pretty lame relationship. Honestly, it's all about trust, right? Well, you're now both guilty of breaking that trust, and it's gonna take a while to rebuild that. Your best bet is to learn a hard lesson and move on for now. You've got some changes to make before you're ready for another relationship.

#44 Reality Bites

The problem: For weeks you've been chatting with your on-line crush for hour after hour every single day. And now he/she finally wants to meet you. Problem is, you've been totally lying about what you look like. You know he/she likes tall people, so you added seven inches to your height.

The goal: To get out of a face-to-face hookup.

Before you begin: You know all the rules about meeting an on-line crush. The first rule is don't do it. The second rule is to remember that this all happened on-line (otherwise known as Fantasyland). You can't expect anything much better than reality on-line.

Give up on this crush. It's extremely unlikely that it will work out.

Consider the fact that if you lied so hard, he/she probably lied, too. This may make it easier to convince yourself that you had nothing in common in the first place.

For maximum karma points, come clean. Tell the truth. Chances are this will kill the "relationship," which might sting, but this sucker was doomed from the get-go, and your conscience will be clear.

4 **If you can't** stomach telling the truth, have your fake-ass alter ego dump him/her, then kill your screen name and disappear from his/her on-line world, leaving him/her no way to contact you. Then, later, like in a few weeks or so, attempt to get to know him/her, in real life this time.

5 **Wise up.** Hanging out on-line is cool and all, but you are still responsible for things you say while you're there. Lying on the Internet is what the Internet is usually all about, but just because it's the Internet doesn't mean you can expect to get away with it.

The bottom line: Don't meet up with people you've only met on-line. It's stupid, not just because whoever you meet won't be what you thought they were, but because there's a massively huge chance whoever you meet will be someone who wants to hurt you. Therefore, don't hook up with people you've only met on-line. And not only that, don't share any info on-line that lets anyone know too much about you and where you are. Like, no sharing your address, phone number, stuff like that. If you do find yourself with someone you don't know getting too cozy or scary or threatening, get the cops on your side ASAP. Got it?

#45 The Mole

The problem: You bust your little brother posing as you on-line and IM-ing your crush about all kinds of inappropriate things, some of them embarrassingly true.

The goals: To contain the leak and punish your kin.

Before you begin: Prioritizing your response is essential at this time. First, contain and control the damage done by your sibling. You have only a small window of time to take care of this. Brother punishment can happen at any time. In fact, the longer you delay the inevitable, which he knows is coming, the harder he'll squirm. Which is way more fun for you.

Move him out of the way and take over the IM. Immediately explain to your crush what is going on. If possible, call your crush and explain that your kid brother was on-line for the last twenty minutes and that you've been in the shower. Don't go over with your crush exactly what your kid brother said because that will make you seem like you have something to hide. Instead mention how annoying your sib is, then change the subject. If you are completely nonchalant about it, chances are he/she will be, too.

Read carefully exactly what was said in the IM, and save it in several places on your hard drive. Do not, as suggested above, mention any of the topics to your crush, because if you bother to protest a particular allegation, you'll raise suspicions about it. But hang on to the evidence just in case an unwanted conversation or, worse, confrontation does arise out of the contents of the IM. You may need the specific details someday.

Never bring up the situation again with your crush. If you're lucky, the incident will fade well into the background of your crushdom and may even serve to bring you two closer together.

Do bring the situation up, emphatically, with your brother. However, don't beat the daylights out of him. Violence won't work. Tempting as it is, it only turns things even more sour than they already are. (Although a small, openhanded, satisfying smack upside the head won't really hurt anyone. Don't tell your parents where you heard that.)

Threats, however, are shown to be remarkably effective on younger siblings. Don't threaten to kill 'em or anything like that, because you won't, and that just amounts to an empty threat. Instead, use something extremely real, like telling everyone how they wet the bed until age seven or pulling down their pants at their birthday party. Sound childish? It has to be: You're dealing with a child. Prey on their concrete fears.

6 **Sibling-proof** your computer:

a. Change your password, frequently.

b. Have passwords for your operating system as well as your on-line service (and everything else on your machine, for that matter), and use them.

c. If you use a laptop, hide the power source and battery, in different and frequently changing places, whenever you're not using it.

d. If, and only if, you think it will directly help you, alert a parent that you're under siege. Work with him or her to create a plan to keep your kid brother's speedy little fingers to his own keyboard. Understand, however, that having a parent on your side often becomes a burden in the long run. Make this decision carefully.

The bottom line: Believe it or not, most people, including your crush, understand how annoying younger siblings can be, and they only rarely hold it against you. The more you make this a big deal, the bigger a deal it will become. But if you just let it go and ignore it as best you can, chances are it will fade quickly.

#46 Intelligence Leak

The problem: You discover that your completely embarrassing on-line diary—the one you checked the "keep it private" box for when you created it—has been hacked into and posted on a bulletin board on the school Web site.

The goal: To minimize exposure and punish the guilty party.

Before you begin: See situation #44.
Having this much attention thrust upon you, while it may sting, might just be a good thing in the long run. Of course, it may not be, too, but hold on to this hope as tight as you can.

Erase the original diary from the site, leaving no obvious record that you've even been involved with doing anything so silly as keeping a diary on-line.

Get your most trusted friend/adviser to ask the school Web site to take down the posting. Do not do this yourself, as it will make people think you care, which will make them think there's something you don't want them to see, which will make them want to see it even more.

Whenever anyone mentions it to you, say, "What are you talking about?"

Conduct a careful, precise, complete, silent investigation into who did it.

a. Write down everyone you know who knew you had the diary. Studies would probably show that most on-line diary-hackers know the victim very well. There's a good chance they even live together. So your suspect is probably on that list.

b. Ask each person on your list about it, in person. Use your instincts to pick up on suspicious behavior that would indicate guilt or lying. (See below.)

c. Discuss with your most trusted friend/adviser. They might have information. Do not, however, ask everyone you know. Keep it quiet.

d. Be patient about your investigation. Don't jump to conclusions—take in all the information slowly and methodically before identifying a perpetrator.

Depending on your relationship to the guilty party, plan an appropriate punishment. If it's a sibling, find a way to profoundly humiliate him/her in front of people he/she really wants to be like. If it's a friend, dump him/her immediately. If it's an enemy of some sort, ignore it completely. (This may seem illogical, but in fact, it's the harshest thing you can do to them. After all, they want you to feel bad, so if you don't, they fail. See?)

6 **Don't bother** writing e-mails to complain to the people on staff at the Web site. They never read those. And even if they do, it will only draw more attention to the situation, and it will keep cropping up even after you've totally let it go.

7 **Consider writing** a lengthy editorial about the evils of privacy invasion on the Web site you used to keep a diary on (see rule #1) or in your school newspaper. It won't stop the snoops, but it might make you feel better. Do it anonymously because you don't want to become the poster child for hacker victims.

The bottom line: Let it go as soon as you can. The more you complain about it or cry injustice, the more seriously people will take the whole thing, and the longer the scandal will last. The sooner you move on, the sooner it will move out of everyone's mind.

How to Tell When Someone's Lying

Trust your gut instinct. Other than having complete proof, it's your best indication. But there are a few things to look for:

1. They don't look you in the eye.

2. They giggle a lot, when that's not what they're really like.

3. They get all fidgety, when that's not what they're really like.

4. They get all red or sweaty all of a sudden when it's not really warm.

5. Their story or excuse is a little too detailed, like they've been practicing it.

6. They act like they don't know what you're talking about or are less interested than they should be.

7. They keep trying to change the subject.

8. They keep making you say stuff like, "I trust you!"

Note: When trying to tell a lie yourself, keep these eight indicators in mind and make sure you don't commit any of them. Mirror practice is valuable, though if you overdo it, you run the risk of violating #5. Never, ever lie without proper preparation.

HYGIENE HORRORS

Is it me? Or does something really smell in here?

#47 Really Sloppy Seconds

The problem: You get the stomach flu (and all its attendant symptoms) . . . on your class trip.

The goal: To suffer in as much silence as possible.

Before you begin: *Okay, you know and I know that this kinda thing happens to everyone. It's nothing to be ashamed of. But let's face it, body function disasters like this are about as humiliating as it gets.*

Get someone in charge on your side, like a teacher or chaperon. All you'll need to say is, "I've got a stomachache and I have to go to the bathroom. REALLY bad." They'll do anything to keep you comfortable and near a toilet for the rest of the day, even if they don't even like you under normal circumstances.

Spend time in the bathroom even if you don't think you really need to go at exactly this moment. The most damning thing you can do is race toward the bathroom with that special look on your face. Instead saunter, gracefully, in that direction well before the crisis stage, and take your time in there.

3 **Run the water** in the sink the whole time you're in there. It may not completely cover all the potty noises you need covered, but it sure can't hurt. Remember, this is not because you're ashamed of the noises you may be making, but it's just polite to anyone outside the room.

4 **If possible**, do whatever you can to fall asleep. Things slow down while you're sleeping. And when you're sleeping, your body's more focused on repairing itself. Most times when you wake up, the episode will be over.

5 **Next time** before the class trip, talk over setting up a prophylaxis plan with your parents—many teens and adults find chewable Pepto to be an essential backpack item.

The bottom line: Believe it or not, most people aren't grossed out by you; they actually feel sorry for you. Not that you should milk this pity, because no one likes a whiner, but it might put your mind at ease to know that they're on your side.

#48 Double Trouble

The problem: You do a #2 at your BF/GF's house, and the toilet begins to overflow.

The goal: To hasten this incident into distant memory.

Before you begin: Take a deep, deep, deep breath, holding your nose if necessary.

1 **Do not panic.**

2 **Do not panic.**

3 **Do not panic.** If applicable, roll your sleeves up really, really high.

4 **If possible** (i.e., if it is free of fake flowers, Hummel figurines, or seasonal dioramas) quickly raise the top of the toilet, plunge your hand into the tank (don't worry, it's clean) and lift the ball cock* up to stop the water from flowing into the toilet. If ball cock has come loose, dig deeper and press closed the plug at the bottom of the tank. Hold it closed until the toilet stops running. This will keep more water from flowing into the bowl.

5 **Look around** for a plunger. Most toilets that back up probably do so frequently, so chances are the family keeps a plunger close by.

6 **If you find** a plunger, fit it carefully over the opening at the bottom of the toilet and very, very slowly depress it to form a vacuum, which feels like a suction-cup-like grip. Then pull back, drawing out any items that have stuck. Repeat as necessary.

7 **If there's no** plunger, look for a brush—you can jam the handle into the opening and perhaps jostle up the clog enough to let water flow. Remember, you'll be washing your hands thoroughly soon enough, so don't be shy.

8 **If you still** can't breach the dam, give up now. Clean up what you can and wash your hands. Twice.

9 **If there's anyone** else in the house, return to your BF/GF with a look of horror on your face. Say something like, "Holy cow! Someone really did a number on your toilet in there. Whew!"

10 **Find an excuse**, and blaze home as fast as possible.

11 **Let him/her** call you. Don't apologize, don't explain, and never, ever bring it up again.

The bottom line: The truth is, most owners of cranky toilets are used to them backing up and know how to deal with it. So while this may seem like one of the most awkward and embarrassing moments of your life, it's probably happened to everyone in the family—including your BF/GF. Really.

*Yes, ball cock is the appropriate name. You have my blessing to repeat this titillating piece of information to all of your friends, most of whom will look at you like you've lost it.

#49 Bubble Up

The problem: You're at home making out with your BF/GF when you burp up a chunk of that hot-'n'-spicy bacon chicken ranch sandwich with curly fries that you scarfed down a couple hours ago with your posse.

The goal: To forge ahead.

Before you begin: When something like this happens, don't try to ignore it. Everyone involved heard, smelled, and probably tasted what just happened. Instead, your MO should be to deal with it in a light, nondestructive way.

1 **Laugh.**

2 **Excuse yourself** to brush your teeth and rinse with mouthwash.

3 **Brush and rinse** again with mouthwash.

4 **Floss**, preferably with a minted dental tape.

5 **One last rinse** with mouthwash.

6 **Chew** a piece of gum, blue or green. Not red or bubble.

7 **Distribute gum** to your make-out partner, and suggest he/she also rinse with mouthwash should he/she wish to.

8 **Stop making out** for a moment and watch TV.

9 **When you can't** stand it any longer, resume making out.

The bottom line: If you both know you're going to be making out later, it's wise to eat the same thing for lunch.

#50 What's That Smell? Oh, It's You.

The problem: It's third period and you decide that there's no way you can let your best friend continue the day smelling the way he/she does. You know, like he/she slept through shower hour for the fourth day in a row.*

The goal: To drop the science, gently.

Before you begin: Carefully consider your subject. Some people pick up on hints better than others. Some people take criticism well, others don't. Take the time to assess the offending party carefully by playing out the confrontation (such an ugly word) in your mind and anticipating the worst. If you believe that the projected net effect over time of telling your friend that he/she stinks will, overall, be detrimental to your friendship, tough it out and hope he/she showers over the weekend. If the projected net effect will be more positive than negative, sally forth.

Commit to making sure that he/she gets told. You have no choice. You'll not only be helping out his/her long-term reputation, you'll also be relieving the rest of your immediate community (i.e., school). After all, this is the 21st century.

We have the means to smell nice, and we should take advantage of them.

2 **Look around** for a surrogate message-bearer. Your ideal play is to mastermind the information transfer without actually having to participate in it. However, this is a long shot, since you're the only one with any *cojones* around here. (Right?)

3 **Attempt hints.** Some might include "Smell my new shower gel! Isn't it great?" Or "Wow, someone's got B.O.!" If they don't get "Didn't you have any hot water this morning?" then you're going to have to get specific, perhaps even brutal.

4 **Find some private** time in a private space. Bathrooms are good. (Check underneath the stall doors.) Far reaches of the school lawn are good. The car is good. (Be sure to glance at the back seat first to make sure the coast is clear.)

5 **Be clear**, be quick, be gentle. "Dude, you are kickin'!" has worked for me in the past. Follow it up with a laugh to defuse the situation, and immediately change the subject. They will get the message.

The bottom line: *Thankfully, people generally only have to be told that they stink once. But someone has to be the one to do the deed. You are the one. Commend yourself on your civic-mindedness, your sense of duty, and your courage.*

*Note: This also applies to overscented friends. You know, the ones who buy into that whole designer-imposter "If you like Giorgio, you'll love Primo!" thing.

Oh, it's me!

Five ways to ensure that you're not the one with the offensive odor:

Shower thoroughly. Every day.

Spot-check frequently. A quick underarm sniff can be executed anywhere you have even two seconds of privacy. (Be speedy about it, and don't get busted. Appearing to be unsure is only slightly less offensive than being the one who reeks. Think of it like picking your nose: It's only slightly less offensive than having a big ol' booger.)

Dried sweat stinks. Keep this maxim in mind whenever considering foregoing the postworkout shower.

Use clean towels whenever possible. There is no swifter way to end up smelling like ass than drying off with a funky towel.

Keep additional scents to a minimum. (If you use a scented soap and/or shampoo, consider blowing off the cologne. Less is usually more when it comes to smelling good.)

So there you have it. A blueprint to surviving the hell that is the teen years. I hope you've learned something. Like, don't puke in the car. And if Dad's wearing a particularly embarrassing outfit, hide. And if you find yourself sporting wood in Biology class, you won't be the first.

But I also hope you learned to have a big fat laugh at yourself. I say this, and I mean it: Taking life too seriously will make it suck. You gotta roll with the punches, and find a little amusement wherever you can...no matter how bad things get. A little humor can make any situation a little better.

So hang in there, and have a little fun. After all, you're a teenager. When are you ever going to have this much fun again?

Later,

Tucker

8/16